argonauta

BY
DEBORAH A. M. PHILLIPS

Copyright © 2014 by Deborah A. M. Phillips
First Edition – October 2014

ISBN
978-1-4602-4332-9 (Hardcover)
978-1-4602-4333-6 (Paperback)
978-1-4602-4334-3 (eBook)

All rights reserved.

No part of this publication may be reproduced in any form, or by any means, electronic or mechanical, including photocopying, recording, or any information browsing, storage, or retrieval system, without permission in writing from the publisher.

Excerpt(s) from GIFT FROM THE SEA by Anne Morrow Lindbergh, copyright © 1955, 1975, copyright renewed 1983 by Anne Morrow Lindbergh. Used by permission of Pantheon Books, an imprint of Knopf Doubleday Publishing Group, a division of Random House LLC. All rights reserved.

Produced by:

FriesenPress
Suite 300 – 852 Fort Street
Victoria, BC, Canada V8W 1H8

www.friesenpress.com

Distributed to the trade by The Ingram Book Company

There are in the beach world certain rare creatures, like the Argonauta, who are not fastened to their shell at all. It is actually a cradle for the young, held in the arms of the mother argonaut, who floats with it to the surface, where the eggs hatch and the young swim away. Then the mother argonaut leaves her shell and starts another life.

– Anne Morrow Lindbergh

For

Natalie Thea

maude

It was the voice of Pierre Elliot Trudeau, which brought Maude back to the present. Something about the War Measures Act, bombings, and the Front de la Liberation du Québec; otherwise known as FLQ terrorists. Whatever the Prime Minister said, it was enough to jar her from the delirium of sleep. She sat up, stretched over to the mahogany table, shut the radio off, then slid back deep into the brown leather couch and tried to recapture in her mind anything that might resemble the past. Like a slow film, thoughts flowed between Westmount, lunch at the Ritz with her parents, Christmas at the Chateau Frontenac, and Saturday afternoons at Ogilvy's with her sisters. Those years had been lived in a fever of expectation.

The phone rang. If it hadn't been hanging in the kitchen, she might have reached for it. Instead, the flying canoe suspended from the wooden rafters of the ceiling reminded her that she was not in her own home. A set of prints depicting Austrian black cocks hung above the mantelpiece, a carving of a capercaillie perched behind a small two-seater sofa, and a large, moody painting of the same bird, amid winter trees, lurked nearby. The only place untouched by the wild was the mezzanine located just behind the canoe.

She sat up, leaned forward against the back of the couch, and gazed out the living room window towards the dark, rough waters of the St. Lawrence. At the deepest end of this body of water, lay a world so rich in colour and marine life that divers could easily imagine they were at the bottom of the Caribbean. She'd read this in one of those guidebooks promoting the wonders of Québec. When she heard the sound of the horse hoofs coming from the paved road around the lane, Maude glanced at her watch. Three o'clock and the carriage tours were still operating in Murray Bay. Tourists lingered even in late October, in spite of the bleakness and lack of color on the landscape. Only the strokes from an artist's brush could bring to life the tenderness of the region now. This panorama annually drew to Murray Bay an assortment of artists, potters, writers, and anyone else looking for a refuge. At this time of the year, you had to capture the dramatics of the earth; lush with a variety of vegetation, rolling hills, and the uniqueness of beach waters filled with white belugas in other ways than actually seeing it.

The phone rang again. *God, who is it this time? My sisters? Not likely.* They would not call now, not today. Karin, daughter number one, would be fuming, and Gillian, her middle sister, would be wrapped in analysis. As they filtered through the maze she had created, it would take a few days before the truth would be confronted. Maybe it was Aunt Grace. Before Maude had to return to her studies in music therapy, her aunt asked her to come back to Murray Bay to work in the gallery for the summer.

Reluctantly, Maude left the comfort of soft leather but stayed away from the phone. Instead, she walked through the hallway towards the front door and opened it, slowly peering around the wooden door to see whether the estranged mallard, nestled against the house earlier that afternoon, was still there. When she arrived from the gallery, the animal appeared undisturbed and oblivious to its unnatural surroundings, and she could not help but wonder why the yellow-billed visitor had not so much as moved his shiny green head or ruffled a white feather when she unlocked the door. Should she leave it open? A duck waddling through this hundred-year old house seemed to fit. Rooted in the historic past, life in Murray Bay moved at a snail's pace, with no sense of time, unscathed by the political unrest and the bombings that were taking place in the rest of the province. Maude had shuddered at the television images of the recent raid on a home in Westmount, a block from where she had grown up. Three hundred and fifty pounds of dynamite hidden in a basement were discovered just before her arrival in Murray Bay. The police were calling it a major breakthrough in the campaign against the weed of terrorism growing in Montreal. The intensified riots at the university, the fires, and the threats of violence on the part of the FLQ, had made her choice to leave the city seem right at the time.

She looked again for the mallard. Vanished. *Obsessed with a duck*, she thought. But it wasn't the bird that had sent her to the couch in midday. On the floor lay the newspaper, exactly where she had thrown it. *Seaside Story Continues* – her picture conveniently placed between the fragile, red-headed woman with dark glasses, and the inserted photo of her adopted mother, Elle Digby, taken when she had won an award for a feature article – *Cross Border Baby Sellers*. Hovered over them was the face of a male with a question mark over the name: Finn Cavanagh. The story continued to the second page, with more pictures and details about Maude's family, other histories that she recognized, and some she had never seen before.

October 15th, 1970:
From The *Star* Editor– Seaside Story Continues

Yesterday's skilful roundup netted a cache of suspects possibly implicated in the recent operations of the FLQ. Several notable faces seen in the jail halls bring to the spotlight events from the past that may have a viable link to the present. Some readers may recall the series of interviews in 1950, with the Irish dissident Finn Cavanagh, by Star reporter Elle Digby from the seaside village of Murray Bay, about Cavanagh's involvement with the Resistance Network. Twenty years later, the daughter of the deceased reporter, Maude Digby, was brought in for questioning along with Québeçoise artiste Anna Tougas, who is known to have close ties with Finn Cavanagh. Police have stated they are seeking more information from both women in connection with the kidnapping of James Cross and Pierre Laporte.

"They are going to ask for details but you don't have to answer to anyone," Anna yelled when they were taken to the police station.

"I can look after myself," she said, while having the distinct feeling that she could not.

When the police took her in for questioning, it was Sunday afternoon, the day after she had gone to meet her birth mother. They were met with a flurry of activity at the jail. There was no way of distinguishing those who were being interrogated, from those protesting and demanding that the raids stop. Maude recognized several reporters from the *Star*. Intermingled in all the commotion with journalists and cameramen, phones rang continuously. And there were voices, like dogs barking; demanding, frustrated, and loud. For a moment she couldn't remember what had happened. A flash of light jolted her back to reality. A reporter demanded to know why she was there.

Someone recognized her. "Aren't you the daughter of Robert and Elle Digby?"

"Bloodhounds," Robert had said so many times. "We are hounds that won't be satisfied until we are fed."

Cameras flashed, then more chaos. Anna was abruptly ushered into another room, leaving Maude alone in front of the mob. She felt the grip of a hand on her arm.

"Let's get out of here," a deep voice came from behind, and she was led to an interrogation room.

Two English detectives standing behind an old wood table were waiting for her. There were no greetings, or formal intros.

"Are we to conclude, Miss Digby, that you have taken it upon yourself to do some of your own reporting?" His hair was short, dark, and greasy, his face strewn with pockmarks. He was overweight and the wrinkled suit and white shirt stained with coffee couldn't help but accent his protruding stomach.

The young detective in a leather jacket, with long unevenly cut hair, sat down and spoke. "We have been informed of certain activities of a particular cell and know that among those kidnappers of James Cross there was an Anglophone from McGill. Do you know who that could be?"

Why ask her? Do you protect someone you don't know but were supposed to know because this person was responsible for bringing you into the world? What was Anna saying in the other room?

"What about Anna Tougas? She's married to this guy, you know that much? She puts on airs of the innocent artist selling her work on Grand Allée, but we have been watching her for years."

They were married – her biological mother and father. Was it that simple? Anna was only protecting her husband?

Before she could answer, the door opened and another detective entered the room. In a lowered voice he gestured to the other two, leaving Maude to ponder whether she would say she was investigating her own story, or tell them that these two people, the artist and the separatist, were her newly discovered flesh and blood.

"Anna Tougas says that you went to see her with the sole purpose of buying art. Is that correct – that you are working in a gallery in Murray Bay and that you have come to collect an order that was made by your aunt?"

"I'm managing the gallery while she is in Europe. My aunt is interested in showing some of this collection."

"Well, this woman may be the *famous artiste* but she's a suspect in protecting some dangerous people."

"I know nothing about this," Maude replied.

"Are you aware of the danger developing in this province?" the younger detective asked quietly.

"Well I never thought that I'd be in a police station this morning," she said clearing her throat. "I have done nothing."

"There is no reason for us to keep you but for your own sense of well-being, we would suggest that you refrain from traveling on your own and that you keep company with someone other than this woman."

So that was it, in a span of a week, Maude felt she had lived years. She studied the front page of the newspaper again. Everything you thought you knew about yourself unravels. The holy relic of identity concealed in an envelope rips open.

"Amending birth certificates is not what we are called to do," the Mother Superior had told her when she showed up at the Convent of the Ursulines. "Have we been divinely appointed to protect fabricated stories?"

The Ursulines were divided on how to handle the secret facts behind the newborns and their birth mothers. They were unjustly viewed as providing a place of punishment and not of refuge. Mother Superior tried to understand that these girls, not women, did love their babies, or at least she thought they all did. "But honestly. How could they think they could possibly keep them?" she asked.

By the end of the conversation, Maude had what she wanted. She left, anxiously clutching a piece of paper bearing the names of her biological parents, and the nun who escorted her to the door wished that the paper had stayed sealed in the cave beneath the convent. It was unusual to identify the birth parents, but in this case, with both adopted parents deceased, Mother Superior had authorized the release of the original document.

> "Born in Québec City, on June 23, 1950, baptized June 28th, 1950. Released for adoption June 30, 1950 by natural mother and placed for adoption on July 2nd, 1950 with Robert and Elle Digby. Biological mother, Anna Tougas, unmarried. Religion, Roman Catholic, student at the Soeurs de la Miséricorde Convent. Biological father Finn Cavanagh, Irish Protestant descent."

Words could not describe how she felt walking out with the information. Twenty years after the day of your birth, you are handed the details. It took several weeks before the numbed state seemed to break enough for her to contact her birth mother.

Anna Tougas lived alone at #17 Rue du Parloir, a tiny street dominated by the Ursulines Convent line, with a row of town houses two blocks from where she'd deposited her child, twenty years ago. She answered her door, dressed in layers of wool and ankle-length mohair, which trimmed her black, laced-to-the-knee boots. Maude was ushered into the smell of paints and bins of stretched canvases.

Anna stood in the midst of her creative paraphernalia, as if she had waited all her life for this moment to let the cork burst on the secret she'd carried for twenty years. "Here is where the trouble started," she said, sorting through a pile of newspapers. "It began with a mildly socialist group – the Resistance Network. Maybe you know about it?" She handed Maude a newspaper. "Most likely not. But at the time, revolutions were stirring everywhere." She pointed to an article on page three entitled – *The Answer.*

> *As a people, French Canada is an almost entirely proletarian colony, occupied by a colonial bourgeoisie, whose language and culture are different from theirs. The answer; 'the absolute independence of Québec' is a precondition for the building of socialism; a Québec brand of socialism, adapted to the particular conditions of North America....*

"Well, after that," Anna took the paper back, "Finn, your father, became a target of investigation; a foreigner from Belfast with a bad influence. Who could have predicted when he came to study law in Montreal, that he would attract a lot of young minds? My parents knew his family and so he spent many Sundays at our dinner table. I was completely taken with him." She lit a cigarette. "By the way, he wants to meet you."

Too exhausted to go anywhere, Maude spent that night with Anna. When she woke the next morning, it was to a new reality.

She wondered about the ease of slipping into another self – was it possible for her to take on a double identity?

She inspected the room in Anna's house as if it were a shrine; the peony-flowered carpet, the lace curtains woven with bicycles and birds, the chintz-covered chair, and the armoire in need of refinishing. A jumbled array of mementos and photos hung on wallpaper, along with lithographs and etchings of old houses. Encased in the walls were rows of oversized books on art, color, knitting, quilting, pottery, and tapestry. So different from what lined the walls of her adopted mother's attic office; images of the events and stories she had captured as a journalist. It was always about the press. Elle Digby was more at home with the newspaper than with the ladies who lived on the Circle, in Westmount.

Maude followed every detail in the room, until her eyes landed on a black and white photo of three people in front of the Frontenac. She recognized Anna, with a woman she thought could have resembled a younger Elle, and a male, she imagined to be Finn.

She wanted to escape, down the stairs, out the door as fast and as far away from ever knowing anything. But it was too late for that wasn't it? Within twenty-four hours her life was an open book spread across the pages of the province.

karin

few ever gain such a depth of knowledge about people they have no personal relationship with, Karin Digby surmised while scanning the medical notice board. By the time a patient's autopsy results were finalized, you knew more secrets than even the family members. It's what you learn after death that gives the past such a heavy weight; not something she had given any thought to before entering medical school. Her fingers searched her lab coat for gum as they brushed against crumpled newsprint; a reminder that she had a family secret of her own. At this moment, instead of standing in hospital scrubs in the late night, she longed to trade places with her middle sister. Gillian, the remote distant type, who preferred fossils to living souls, had planted herself in Miguasha, a remote corner of the province that had held no attraction for Karin when life used to be normal. She wished their last conversation had not ended so abruptly.

"Our lives have changed, Gillian, but that would be hard to notice from the Gaspé," she had yelled into the phone. Her sister hung up.

Karin had always believed that Gillian liked to float outside family life. She stayed uninvolved, picking and choosing when she would participate, never feeling the necessity to give back an ounce. She was the opposite of Maude, sister number three they liked to call her, who could descend to seriousness in a moment, if that was needed. Maude would listen and sympathize with anyone – but was there anything solid about someone who could go and find her birth mother, then wind up in jail and on the cover of the newspaper with her?

Karin headed to the student lounge, opened the fridge, saw no possibilities, went to her locker, grabbed her coat, and proceeded through the halls. A nurse wheeled a bassinette into the nursery. For several moments, Karin peered at the newborns through the thick pane of glass; three wrapped in pink and four in blue. How had this choosing of colours, pink and blue, come about? She gathered her straight black hair and twisted the elastic around her fingers to bring it into a tighter ponytail as she read the names on the bassinets – Elizabeth, Pascale, Madeleine. *No nameless baby in pink, Mother.* In her mind, she followed her adopted mother Elle Digby's steps; questioning everyone on staff about infectious diseases inside the hospitals of Québec, side-tracked to the nursery, snapping photos, then focusing on the one baby with no name. Breathless, Karin clutched her throat. Since her parents had died, it happened without warning. Sometimes in the middle of taking a patient's history, images of her own come up.

Family Status: Parents – journalists, deceased in plane crash while covering a story in Northern Québec. Siblings: two sisters –

Gillian – a package deal rescued from international baby-selling ring in Montreal. Maude – a rescue from the Ursulines, Québec City.

Chief complaint: twice orphaned, no chance of rebirth.

> *Cross border babies get a proper start in life – lovely babies for adoption; excellent health background and healthy bodies.*

Developmental milestone, "a proper start"; three words that had changed the way she felt about herself. She was twelve when she read them. Her mother had been sued for writing about young girls, exploited because they were in desperate circumstances and bullied into giving up their babies. The story uncovered a thriving baby-selling ring. Childless couples from New York City had paid a whopping $10,000 package for the deal – smuggling expenses to cross the border and a fake birth certificate, with baby included. Her father, Robert, a med-school drop-out turned writer, had interviewed the cabbies, waitresses, and hotel clerks who received fifty dollars for solid tips on pregnant unmarried girls coming from Québec's rural areas. One of those young women from the Gaspé, who was about to give birth, was most likely Gillian's mother – at least that's what Karin believed since Gillian was so attached to the region.

"Sometimes, life stories get altered from the beginning," Elle used to tell them.

How Karin was named, the date and hour of her birth, and the place where she arrived on Planet Earth never mattered for her. She had accepted the 'no-name wrapped in pink; negotiated and brought home,' family romance, never straying on to any sort of venture into her background. Why would she? She had Robert, a father she adored. As for her adopted mother, when you arrive into a household because someone thrives on rescuing babies, there never seems to be the right time to revise your story, although she probably could have. Having the answers, meant you had to deal with them.

"I want the Baby in Pink," Elle had casually announced to Robert over supper one night, twenty-some years ago.

"For Christmas or your birthday?" he asked, with no serious intentions.

"I want that baby and I'm not letting her go off to one of those Duplessis' orphanages."

It had been that simple. A no-name orphan wrapped in pink, negotiated with an amended birth certificate, an altered history or a proper start, however you labeled it. What difference did blood ties make, if birth parents were so eager to give up babies? Until now, Karin had embraced the life handed to her. Or at least she thought she had.

"Can you imagine having one of those waiting for you every night? " a voice whispered. Her classmate leaned against the glass pane of the nursery. Dark-haired Jenny; a small, confident, English girl, who spoke French and Italian, with the brains for science and genetics, now nearing thirty and soon to be married. She had it all and Karin sometimes hated her for it.

"Never," she lied. "Not in a million."

"They're looking for extra help in Emerg – more hours if you want them."

"I'll think about it, I need to get something to eat."

What difference would it make if she worked around the clock? Since Maude had declared her days of double existence over, everything that had already upset their lives had become worse.

"Don't get too hung up on those babies, Jen."

Karin left the nursery and headed for her car. She stopped at a water fountain to wash down pills.

"No one's ever ready for this kind of death," friends and relatives all said after her parents' deaths. "You need to get some help, perhaps therapy."

Instead she had opted for the Valium. Only for now, she told herself. Though now might be a good time for that therapy, since she actually had something other than death of her parents to talk about. She straightened up, looked down the corridor, and decided against it. She did have other options. She could continue her readings for the neonatal screening program for Tyrosinemia – a rare genetic disorder that attacks the liver, especially in young children.

Ever since she'd watched helplessly with the parents, as three-year-old Myriam died of the disease, Karin had thought she wanted to be part of the research team to identify affected newborns. Good intentions aside, that wasn't going to happen either. Tonight her mind couldn't absorb anything. Or just maybe it was because the last time she'd seen Maude was in Murray Bay, at a benefit concert for the disorder. Karin had gone to support the cause but she'd had another motive for driving to Murray Bay that late-summer weekend. She'd been determined to talk some sense into her sister before Maude went through with her plans to contact her birth mother.

Futile in every way, the evening had turned out to be a waste of her time. Not only was Maude headstrong on going to Québec City to meet the woman, she'd spent the evening flirting with a French doctor Karin had trained with. Dr. Yuri Rousseau prepared medics for war zones. He also worked shifts in Emergency Medicine. Maude had no idea of the horrid encounters Karin had endured during several rotations he'd supervised. All Karin could think about, as her sister chatted endlessly, was how he had humiliated her during her last clinical rotation.

"You might wish to focus your career in a pathology lab, removed from any direct contact with patients," he'd told her after a particularly gruelling night in ER during an endless stream of ambulances transporting trauma victims and patient walk-ins.

The fresh autumn air and biting wind felt surprisingly good. It was Sunday night. Karin had been at the hospital almost fourteen hours. She unlocked the door to her car, got in, and turned on the radio. A steady male voice calmly explained the details of the most recent FLQ communiqué. As she listened, she tried to conceive a face to match the words.

"A letter to Robert Bourassa from Pierre Laporte, pleading for his life, has now been made public."

> "My dear Robert," wrote the Minister, "there is no doubt in my mind that this is the most important letter I have ever written. My life is in your hands. If there were nothing more to it than that and if that sacrifice might bring good results, it could be considered. But what we have here is a well-organized escalation of violence, which will not end until the political prisoners are released. After me there will be a third hostage, then a fourth, and a twentieth. It's better to act right away and so avoid a useless bloodbath and panic. If the political prisoners are allowed to leave, I have absolutely no fears for my own personal safety or that of others who might follow. It could be done quickly, for I see no reason why it should drag on and keep me dying by inches in the place where I am being held. Decide whether I am to live or die. I'm counting on you and I thank you. Best Wishes. Pierre Laporte.

As she drove onto the Metro, she spotted the historic brick building that housed the *Star* where both her parents had worked. Robert and Elle – they always called them by their first names, just one of the many oddities in the family – had met while fighting over whose work would get front-page coverage, back in 1949. Elle's story on the *Ladies of the Sceptre;* a history of the five queens who had reigned before the upcoming young Elizabeth would be crowned, won over Robert's piece on a rising baseball star named Mickey Mantle.

"Twenty cover stories on baseball in one year are enough," Elle had argued with her editor, a gross exaggeration that worked, and a professional habit Karin had learned over the years.

Elle and Robert married six months later, on a snowy afternoon in a tiny eighteenth-century chapel in Murray Bay where the family summered every year. They bought a house in Westmount. Growing up in the elite community, Karin discovered that her mother was more at home with the newspaper than with the other women of what had become known as 'the Circle'. Elle refused to fit into the British enclave that viewed French, as she termed it, 'a landscape to be traversed en route to Knowlton in the summer or Sainte-Agathe in the winter.'

Karin steered the car off the ramp and headed towards the exit to the family home. *Some perspective time,* she thought. In truth, she felt lost and over-emotional.

She drove through the groomed yards of Westmount. Even in the dreariness of late October, they were a constant reminder of the secluded life she had taken for granted. Her adopted mother may have been embarrassed by the overbearing English flavour of their neighbourhood, but Karin loved it.

She swung the car off the main street, drove carefully into the lane, and parked behind Sophie's Volkswagen. Turning the key to the door, she noticed the cracked paint and dirt around the doorframe and window. Inside, the house appeared to be deteriorating with that same intensity. The only life left was her mother's longtime friend, who had now become like a bird of passage that stayed too long.

Sophie Frachette was sitting at the table, sorting through photographs. With Sophie still hanging around since the accident, which had been over a year ago, Karin imagined she was waiting for one of them to crack. Well, why then wasn't she with Maude in Québec City or wherever she was? Or in the Gaspé, in that 150-year-old house she'd restored after being jilted by a lover. Growing up through the years, that house had seemed to fit more with Gillian than the Tudor graystone in Westmount.

No tantrums, Karin told herself. If only that numb feeling would kick in, it might help her manage Sophie's demanding presence and those awful baggy jeans and sloppy sweater she wore. Instead of opening the refrigerator, Karin opted for the liquor cabinet.

"I wasn't expecting you," Sophie said, "or I would have prepared a meal. What about a sandwich and some tea?"

"I need something a bit more substantial than that," Karin responded from the dining room. Sophie had never been the perfect guest. Domestically speaking, she was a dead loss and Karin's mother had spent more time picking up after her than the rest of them. She was good for making lists and arranging their annual photo sessions, but that was about it.

"She's a commie," her father once said.

"Just because she has her own ideas about politics?" her mother argued.

Other than the fact that whenever Sophie was with her mother, her presence rekindled so much life, Karin could never figure out the ties between these two women, which had lasted for so many years.

"Did you see the paper?" Sophie was standing in the arch of the dining room now.

"How could I miss it?" Karin poured herself a drink. "Spare me the details, I'm not interested." She stopped in front of Sophie with a look of disdain. "I saw their faces, on the front page. Isn't that enough?"

She waited for Sophie to reply, but then drew back and smiled thinly.

"I'm going to study." She headed to the den where for the most part of her growing years, her parents spent their winter evenings in a welter of newsprint – a babble of information they'd called it. They would seize on topics before people knew they should be concerned about them.

She could hear Sophie from the kitchen banging pots and pans nervously re-organizing as she did since the girls were now on their own. Karin wondered how long she would hang around. It wasn't like they were children. They didn't need her or even want her.

Things looked the same in the family study but felt different. On the walls were photographs of her parents shooting ptarmigan on Alaskan glaciers and catching sailfish in Mexico. Their love of adventure had been infectious.

Elle had followed the path of her mother. "I like a difficulty," Karin's grandmother would say. Lilly McGrath had been passionately engaged in accomplishments. She had walked across Africa in the 1930s, mapping the language of the Congo Basin for the Royal Geographic Society. A strong, courageous woman, she'd encouraged her daughter to be even more exploratory. It seemed like war, disaster, upheaval, and discomfort brought out the best in some women like Karin's mother and grandmother. They enjoyed taking risks. "I'd love to play bridge and go to parties but how does one do that when there's a world out there?" This was her mother's favourite line.

Karin stared at the photos. There was no sense of comfort anywhere, in spite of the fact that nothing had been moved or displaced since that horrid day when the call had come about the crash. The den was always a degree too cold, especially before winter. On the desk lay one of those glass globes that when shaken, sprinkles snow over a country village. *She sees Robert turning it up and down, back up and back down; a habit he has when searching for words. Wearing his grey, wool sweater, Robert glances at her standing at the entrance, mumbles, "Hi," and continues to type.*

She has just received news of her acceptance into medical school.

He mumbles again. "It's a start."

She wonders how he can say such a thing, since it was he, the medschool dropout, who had encouraged her to pursue medicine.

"So much schooling." Her mother comes in and caresses her hair. "Are you sure you can hold on for eight years?"

"I know what I can or can't do," she says, waiting for her father's words. He will say something else, won't he? There will be more. She waits but there is silence. He is preoccupied. He will eventually come around; after his deadline he will let her know she's measured up. It is his way. It doesn't matter. She believes in him.

The family procession through the room continued.

"I don't give a damn about what he thinks," Gillian had yelled the time Robert opposed her trips to Miguasha.

"She's a commie or she's in love with them." His flippant remarks about Sophie's involvement in anything political were frequently voiced.

"So if you have strong opinions or different ideas, you're a communist," Elle repeatedly protested.

But he'd insisted there were ties somewhere; she'd been around too many riots and campaigns. Sophie was hiding something.

Karin took the vial of pills from her pocket, loosened the cap and shook the lot of them out into her palm. She put her hand to her mouth, pushed them in, gagged and swallowed the vodka from her glass. Some spilled down the sides of her mouth. The telephone rang. Nauseous, she left the den and went upstairs to her parents' ensuite where she took her clothes off and headed for the bathtub.

It was through photography that Sophie Frachette had come to understand the Digby girls. Years in the darkroom, enlarging each child's image, had somehow allowed her to believe that she had a place in the details of their lives. Only time would permit her to know if this was to their benefit, for the idea was based entirely on the lens and film. As she sat at the desk of her friend's attic office in Westmount, browsing through a collection of simple events like holidays, birthday parties, and changing seasons, she was reminded, once again, that she was helpless, except for the photos.

Take Gillian. Her eyes confronted the camera with suspicion, apprehension, and reserve. Previously, Sophie had never considered herself to be anything more than friend, photographer, and godmother to Gillian. And now more than ever, Sophie would rather return home to the land's end for picking up the shipwrecked, otherwise known as the Gaspé. Run aground may have been the way others would have described her when she'd made the choice to plant herself at the end of the peninsula in the late '50s. After her one failed attempt to fit into a long-lasting relationship, she'd amazed even herself when she revealed to Elle how those words 'for better or worse' no longer appealed to her.

"Babies," said her friend. "You'll be too busy to even think like this if you consider having a baby."

"So the baby is the key to staying linked till death do us part?"

"What's wrong with that? You're being very self-centred," Elle replied.

Is that what women were supposed to do? Have babies to help them keep a promise? Sophie felt stifled at even the thought that a baby could actually make an elusive, independent woman become suddenly committed and maternal.

Now, twenty-some years later, the truth about maternal connection with her best friend's children had kicked in. It wasn't reciprocated and she had to live with that, except for Miguasha. Thankfully, both Gillian and she had found their own source of comfort in this carved coastline, small coves, high sea cliffs, national parks, and of course the lighthouses. Not even the cold winters bothered them. Sophie worked at photographing the matriarchal life spans of whale pods in the waters around Tadussac; every season yielding a data collection of thousands of negatives to classify and catalogue for trends and patterns. For her, the photos sold enough. It wasn't just to magazines and research documents but the summer tourists proved to be a valuable source of income for her, though a nuisance for others.

At this moment, she longed to go to her own home, yet she had no choice but to stay in Montreal. Never in her wildest dreams would she have supposed the present situation would emerge into this full-scale unearthing of everything her dearest friend, Elle, had so fervently worked to protect.

She continued to sort the photos. Gillian – a tall, athletic figure, blond and with blue eyes; out there digging and itemizing in the baffling world of palaeontology…and poles apart from her older sister. Detached, determined, confident, and very inventive about categorizing people.

Karin, Sophie regarded as a study in torment; a monologue needing to become a conversation. Drama school, not medicine, would have suited those dark, piercing eyes.

She picked up a print of the youngest, Maude – another portrait in contradiction. Maude was either too much light or too much shadow; a free bird in one picture, a portrait of eternal yearning in another. Why or what for, she could not comprehend. A proper start had been offered to this fragile, five-pound redhead at birth. Elle had managed to sign her out of the Ursulines, where she had been placed after her young mother was shipped out of the country to Paris.

Sophie carefully placed the photos of these three young women back into their protective corners.

She dialled the number again for the private residence of Dr. Yuri Rousseau. Sophie was not the least bit intimidated by phoning him at his home or at the hospital – photo journalists have done worse. No response. She considered showing up at his apartment. She was anxious, not because she must pursue the doctor but rather that certain events had begun to unravel impetuously. Her fingers leafed through another stack of papers that she had kept bound in a thick, letter-sized, leather folder. Notes scribbled on hotel letterhead, news articles, and more photos. The story behind the pictures – they should be sorted; '40s '50s and so on. But that would make their lives coherent, wouldn't it? She needed more – perhaps a letter written with explanations; something to be passed on in the event of death. Suppose Elle had realized that in the end, all would be revealed anyway. Was that possible?

Elle, the journalist, and Sophie, the photographer, were at one time an inseparable team. They had met in France, in the city of Fontainebleau, at one of Sophie's exhibitions of photos from the war. Elle had been travelling through Europe, interviewing displaced war victims. She came to the show seeking to write an article on power of the photograph and why it matters. She was immediately drawn to the dramatic imagery in Sophie's work. For six months Elle devoted herself to the exposition and the stories behind the photos. The end result was a feature article in the *New Yorker*. They were stronger together Sophie felt, brilliant, and somehow they managed to believe in themselves and their work.

But the tide turned when Elle received notification from the *Star* to send in her stories and change her focus towards England. Canadians wanted a break from the war stories. Get ready for the coronation and bring it all back to Canada. Either that or find another paper to support her ventures.

By the time Sophie landed in Montreal less than a year later, her friend had done what every woman felt was necessary for completion – she had married. Elle believed unquestioningly that a woman was unfulfilled without it, like the end to a good story. She wed Robert just after he had quit medicine, after one year of internship, to become a writer. In those days that was giving up a lot of prestige but Elle had casually stated, "I admire his determination."

It was unrealistic, Sophie thought. The man skipped through travel writing, sports events, and reviews for spy thrillers. When Sophie was introduced to him, she predicted the differences between them, as a couple, would be as wide as they were long.

She turned the black and white photo over and read; 1951– Elle, Finn, Anna. She remembered the night it was taken.

"Sophie, I need you to come to this interview. It's big…explosive. Oh God, Sophie I can hardly work it." Her friend and co-worker, usually confident, had never seemed so anxious.

"It's huge – not sure how we'll do photos. And leave Robert out of this. He'll be furious if he finds out what's going on. This group is going to stir something in this province that's going to change it completely. We meet at *le Kaf* on St. Henri at six. Some other journalist is supposed to be there from Ottawa. She's got some kind of link in this, other than news interest, something I haven't figured out, yet. Keep the camera in your bag until I say ok."

Sophie knew some things about the Resistance Network. It had started out as a mildly socialist group, influenced by worldwide trends towards decolonization. Like other movements, they had outside help from countries more advanced in their revolutionary strategies, such as Peoples China and Ché Guevara in Latin America. Revolutions stirred everywhere. Latin movements were listening to new voices like Castro. In the Middle East, Arafat's Fatah party and other Palestinian liberation groups were preparing to launch attacks in Israel. She had observed the tactics from the Resistance fighters in France during the Second World War. In Québec, the mood was turning inward towards a new awakening know as distinctiveness. Through song, theatre, and new films, Québecers were finding themselves. The press attentively followed these new voices rising up in the province.

Her own life at the time was in a state of redesign. Unlike other women who had been displaced by the war, she managed to travel on assignment to various rallies and reunited with another journalist, whom she had met with Elle while on assignment in Paris. René Lévesque was now back home in Québec, from his reporting stint in Korea, and was suddenly the new hero in the province. She was working a photo op in the Gaspé where they briefly reconnected and exchanged stories about the war. There were moments she recalled where she caught the chemistry in the eye to eye, whether real or imagined. It was his brilliance that kept her listening to an ideology that seemed to transcend whatever she had heard before.

She wondered how he felt now about the cell in Percé? Or had he imagined at the time, with all the momentum that the independence group was gaining across the province, that someday he would rise to lead it? The mood for decolonization was everywhere. The process was filled with revolutionary romanticism that was more than ready for the birth of a radical movement like the Québec national liberation group now known as the FLQ. The one costly regret in her life was being swept into that romanticism.

Her fingers pressed the black and white photo. The faces of Elle, Finn, and Anna stared back at her. A snapshot has limitations; revealing things from only one angle, she thought. How often it tends to omit the finer details. It was the photographer's task to unmask. That night, not only was the province of Québec in the throes of unrest – so was her best friend. When Sophie walked into *le Kaf* at six-thirty, Elle was seated in a dark corner, completely immersed in conversation with a young, attractive male, who appeared to be accompanied by an even younger female. So young that Sophie wondered if this frail teen might not be a younger sister of someone in that small group of dissidents.

Rising, Elle's sturdy shoulders and light-brown hair gave her an easy, expansive manner and she motioned to Sophie to pull up a chair. A man in his early twenties stood up, introduced himself as Finn Cavanagh, and presented a very pregnant Anna Tougas.

As her eyes lowered and raised at the physical features of the young woman, Sophie made a quick gesture of reaching out to shake hands. Grateful the place was poorly lit so as to hide her obvious unease, she pulled out a chair and quickly sat on the outside of the group.

Finn spoke. "We were just discussing the recent clip in the papers, regarding the low number of influential French bosses around the province."

"My father is one of the very few of course," said the young Anna confidently.

"Yes, but your father does nothing to further the cause of others in this province," Finn interrupted.

"Well he doesn't agree with les Anglais running everything you know," Anna insisted, twisting her fingers around her mane of red curls.

"The point is – what does he do about it?"

"Well I'm sure he would do something if he could."

"What do you think Anna's father should do Finn?" Elle interrupted, pulling a pencil from her bag and opening her notebook.

"Look, it's very obvious that any movement towards change needs strong voices; if he was really concerned, he'd be here tonight." By this time, Finn was moving closer to Elle, shifting his attention completely onto her.

Sophie gazed around the café and wondered how far this small band of dissidents would go. They were more than flirting with the ideals of independence. The three men and two women across from their table appeared to be immersed in the large piece of paper spread across the table, which must have been a map. She recognized the reporter from Ottawa. There would definitely not be any photos taken at this meeting.

"Let's say he was here tonight with you, what would be the plan to move this issue to the front page of the papers?" Elle was pressing now.

Finn cleared his throat and lowered his voice, and sliding closer to Elle almost whispered, "Well, if I was to give a list to an English journalist on all the upcoming proposals and plans, now where would that be going and to what page on the newspaper are we talking about?"

"It really depends on whether or not you've got anything substantial to write about." Elle did a quick raise of her eyebrows and carefully placed her pencil across her notebook. Sophie noticed her eyes shift towards Finn.

Less than a year later, daughter number three entered the Digby household. Unlike the other two babies, Maude could have crossed the threshold through the womb of the woman who was ready to raise her. The passion that had slipped between Finn and Elle that night and the nights to follow could have borne more than a quiver full if nature had been favourable. But this was Anna's baby she chose to adopt, not her own.

Sophie picked up the recent issue of the *Star*. Maude, Elle, and the latest photo of the artist Anna, stunned as usual; not much had changed. The last time she'd seen her, Anna had a brush clenched in her mouth and her painting paraphernalia scattered around her easel, on the beach. What had started as a cloudless summer morning was shifting hour by hour and the wind and the sand would not co-operate. For the second time, Anna packed her paints, brushes, and cloths back into the wooden case and moved higher up onto a sandbank. The tide was dead low, the shoreline a vast flat of sand and sea-muck and Murray Bay, as usual in the heat of summer, was scattered with clam diggers and tourists.

Finn was lying on a blanket, discoursing about painting from real life. "The landscape changes every day – nothing in nature stays the same and that is how you bring life to your painting."

Anna ate every English word that flowed from his Irish mouth. Swallowing them as eagerly as any young protégée enamoured with an idle philosopher, steeped in political science and fluent in French but with an accent so thick she would often shriek hysterically.

"But it must be so much easier to work from still photos," Elle interrupted, picking at an egg salad sandwich.

"You know, fill in the gaps with your imagination. Besides, with this wind and sand shifting hourly, how does one focus?"

Anna forced the easel legs deeper into the mound where she stood, pulled her straw hat into place, and continued to paint, ignoring the comments.

"Sketching things out, then working out the details with paint – wouldn't it have the same, perhaps better, effect? You could add your own style," Elle continued. "Take for example, the thickness in the trunk of that tree over there."

"First you establish if it is awake or sleeping." Finn reached across and poured more wine.

"What, like the tree that sleeps in winter?" Elle sat up and wrapped her arms around her legs.

"Or maybe you make it a Tree of Liberty," Finn said.

"What kind of tree?" Anna turned to him.

"Well naturally you haven't heard of the Tree of Liberty; a simple pine festooned with green ribbons, as a symbol for the rebels – a desire to be free of their Crown masters. Each time a portion of land was recaptured, seized back by local landowners, the tree was burned. But it didn't matter because the seeds and the ideal had planted themselves in the hearts of the Irish men and women and could never be removed. New seeds would be planted and they would grow up to be strong and productive."

Finn Cavanagh talked more about war than anything else, Sophie noted. *He's fighting with his own flesh over here, or does he ever consider Grosse Isle? One assumes the war boy knows his history.*

"We're not at war here – the war is over. Papa says these are post-war days. Besides I'm not interested in painting trees right now," Anna said.

"Call it what he wants, peace over here in Québec doesn't feel that different to me. You're not any freer here. Even your mother and father agree with that. They want to see the Québeçois running their own province. Not les Anglais."

"Well that's one of the things we do have in common." Anna moved away from her canvas. "Both our families hate the English."

A picnic blanket covered with histories, placed together on a political and social landscape that was about to implode.

Sophie put the photos away and poured herself a glass of wine. She turned to the heap of newspaper clippings that had been left in a pile on the corner of the desk – *Lovely Babies for Adoption; Excellent Health Background and Healthy Bodies; Cross Border Babies get a Proper Start – Guest Child; Ladies of the Sceptre – The Coronation* series; *The Death of the Night Watchman.* Elle's keen interest in the FLQ movement had been shaken by that last event. It turned out to be the worst nightmare of her reporting career.

Sophie knew she had no choice now. She picked up the phone. This time she would leave another message for Dr. Rousseau. *Why wasn't your brother arrested?*

gillian

Take a step back in time before humans appeared, before even the first dinosaurs – when this stretch of Gaspé coast was located four degrees south of the equator, on a continent known as Old Red Sandstone. I'm on the edge of a large river, at least 20 kilometres wide, which flows into the Rheic Ocean. It's very hot; there's a forest of enormous ferns, but no trees, no flowers on the edge of the water. There's a little pool on the shore with an absolutely astonishing variety of fish in it. Some have spines, some are covered with armour, notice one in particular; a predator with well-developed fins. I'm not sure but it looks like it's trying to pull itself out of the water to chase a scorpion on the shore.

gillian Digby sat outside the observation centre, listening to the recording for daily visitors, thinking that if someone wanted to escape from it all, Miguasha Park was the place to go, although not many would choose the Gaspé Peninsula in October. Only the diehard fossil hunters would put up with the not-fall-not-really-winter weather that blows cold wind, snow, rain, and hailstones into the cove, all in the same hour. Extreme but expected.

The fact that her summer-tan legs were still covered with blotches and scrapes, or that her hands and feet were scored with cuts, didn't really matter either. Not much would heal out here. It was the centuries of secrets hidden in the grey cliffs on this south shore of the peninsula that drew her. They held life in suspension, like photos fixed in time. Miguasha was now known as one of the best fossil parks in Canada and was about to be named a World Heritage site. Gillian hoped it wouldn't make a huge difference. Already there was some talk about dropping busloads of tourists to dig for several hours at a time, in hopes of turning out more fossils.

Accompanied by the raucous quarrels of nesting gulls, she jumped from the granite ledge and headed towards the circle of tents, assembled to provide shelter for their equipment. Most of their gear was now packed. Too many windstorms had hit the cove where the team had been digging. They had no choice. It was time to leave the site. Gillian planned to move into Sophie's house at Pierre St. Croix, at least until Christmas. She would go just about anywhere but Montreal, but that was until today. Earlier that morning, after another storm hit, they had uncovered what appeared to be a fairly well-preserved, wooden box in the clay-packed soil. Not that unusual in paleo digs, except this one was about to become an issue.

"Interested in the gory life of an old corpse?" Behind her, squinting in the late afternoon sun was the tanned face of her boss, Michel Fortier. Seeing him always made her think of one of those cigarette ads, where the men appeared overly self-possessed. Although she couldn't figure out his age, he was not much taller than her father; five-foot six, muscular with sandy hair, and his English was heavily accented. Gillian wasn't keen that he spoke English to her when everyone else on the team spoke French. He ignored the fact that she was completely bilingual and spoke with no hint of an Anglo accent; the product of her mother's insistence that they grow up with double vision, which translated into think, feel, and speak in both languages.

"Isn't everyone?"

"There's not much in a box of bones that hasn't been figured out already around this area. But for everybody's satisfaction, it's being sent to Montreal to the Laboratoire des Medécine Legale – we'll let the forensic anthropologists examine the contents. By the way, I'd like you to come with me to Montreal. I need an assistant from the team to compile some data while I'm there."

"Is there no one else?"

It was the wrong thing to say. Not just because he had given her this summer-turned-fall job, but he was the director of one of the most important paleo sites in the world. And her sister happened to be staying in his home in Murray Bay; a convenience arranged by her mother's best friend, Sophie. Michel Fortier and the photographer had 'history,' supposedly from time spent together in France. But this year was Gillian's first official job as an assistant with the team and until this moment, the time had been ideal – any interruption, like returning to Montreal, was completely unwelcome.

She cleared her throat. "Who makes the complex decision, anyway, to move a coffin?" It was a feeble attempt to change the mind of someone who had been caught with fossils in Russia, between a murder and gunfights; who had studied fossils at the Natural History Museum in England, and had previously worked at France's foremost research institute: the Centre National de la Recherche Scientifique.

"Not much we can do here," Michel said. "The historic dead require special permission from the coroner to perform the analysis."

She turned, pushing her fingers through her blond curls. "I'll be glad to go." It was the second time this week that she'd said the opposite words to what she was thinking.

"It's not a prison sentence," Michel said, giving her one of those quit-your-whining looks. He left her standing alone amongst the low hanging, misty clouds that were now drifting from the water towards the cliffs.

"Put the coffin in the van," he yelled to a few members from the team. "It will be coming to the airport with us in the morning."

Tension hung in the air; unearthing the dead made everyone uneasy. *Like Maude digging up her own past,* Gillian thought. Until the plane crash, she'd always felt her younger sister possessed brains, but now, left on her own, she seemed abruptly at sea. Genetics aside, searching for parents now could ruin what you had spent so long inventing about yourself. Her sister was obviously lost, Gillian concluded as she turned on the propane stove. She had never felt that way – misplaced at times but never lost. Gillian had tried to reason with Maude again, just last week. She had been passing the morning mopping up water from what must been the tail end of a hurricane on its way through the Atlantic, tediously sorting and labeling the remains of a flattened fish fossil that had scattered, when her sister called.

"Gill, I'm on my way to meet my mother and who knows, maybe a father," Maude announced.

It took several seconds to grasp what Maude meant.

"Can you believe it?" Her sister's voice raced.

"Are you ready for all this truth?" Gillian wanted to know.

"Meeting these people could be like finding a fossil with a story," Maude said.

It was the way the word 'people' came out that irritated Gillian. She would not let 'these people' find their way into her life. It was such a risk. The kettle boiled and she rummaged through some sacks for tea, as she thought about what to say to her sister. One of the team members had brought loose leaves from Africa that she wanted to try.

"You could get hurt," was all she managed to say, as her thumb pressed the dry mix into the tea strainer.

"That's what Karin thinks. Have you two been talking?"

Sharing the same side thoughts as her older sister could never happen. Gillian heard herself say, "I just want you to be careful, you know, check them out first."

That was the other conversation where she never really said what she meant. What she wanted to say was that maybe for now, it was hard to face the fact that if a mother plainly had not wanted you and then patently never regretted giving you up, then how could you possibly think that life would be any better by finding her? She hadn't been able to bring herself to say that but Maude would not have listened anyway. What her sister needed was a shrink. If Elle had to see one while she was alive, then Maude could use one now even more.

The trouble was that no one knew that her mother had a shrink. Gillian was privy to this only because of an argument about Greenland. She had carefully planned the trip to study lobefins that summer, when her mother announced they were going to vacation in Ireland. Her mother's trips were all excuses for research and journalistic pursuits. There would be absolutely no adventure in that. Even her father wasn't going. Not that Gillian cared; ever since she'd told him her future goals included straddling alligators, swimming up to the mouths of whales, and standing in caves filled with bats, he never seemed to speak to her seriously.

"I'm not going," Gillian had announced at the Ritz, one cold Sunday afternoon as the family was seated around their usual table.

"Lobefins – that's the most grotesque excuse I've heard of," Karin said without bothering to look at her. "I've been meaning to tell you about my own plans, Mother."

Karin's timing was off as usual; she could never really figure out what she wanted. Being the oldest gave her the right to bulldoze in whenever she finally made her mind up about anything, so turning the plans into her own was something she did quite naturally.

"Gillian, you are coming. Karin, no arguments," they were told.

Gillian had sulked for two weeks and looked for a way out. But it was the call that had changed everyone's plans. It was the editor from the *Star*, Joe Blackburn.

"There's a flood in the Saguenay and we need someone to go up there. Here's the flight information, tell your parents I'd like them to be on it in the morning. They can fly in and out for the day. Can you pass that on to them, Gill?"

"Sure," she had replied with hopes to encourage them to take it. Running up to her mother's attic office, where she rarely entered, she searched through Elle's papers for a note pad to write on. What she hadn't figured on was finding Elle's private appointment book blocked with: A. Labelle – psychiatrist – Monday at 3:00 p.m. Gillian turned back to the previous week. A. Labelle – 3:00 p.m. The previous was the same and she turned forward to the next Monday – more time blocked for A. Labelle. Today was Monday. Her mother had told them she was at the university library on Mondays, doing research.

Like tilting rocks and finding more than starfish, Gillian believed that a window of opportunity to change her mother's mind had been handed to her. Why was the *Star* reporter seeing a shrink? It couldn't be research, or interviews. Over the years, they had learned the difference between personal and work.

But Gillian never had the chance to figure it out; the chartered flight crashed in the Saguenay before landing. It seemed at the time that the death of her parents created more news than they had ever written when they were alive. That summer the Digby sisters were thrown into a series of shocks and people they didn't know, with plans they had no control over. Now here they were, one year later, scattered across the province. Gillian would not return to Westmount, Karin could not stay away, and Maude's trips to Québec City could only mix her up more than she already was.

The next morning, Gillian sat a few yards from the water and watched the fog roll in across the water. She braced herself against the rough wind and tried not to think about Montreal and what she would do once they had finished delivering the coffin. She had no idea what kind of help Michel wanted. Surely she wouldn't be asked to label the human bones. She picked up her duffle bag and wandered towards the Interpretation Centre where he would be waiting for her. Like most palaeontologists, Michel had a van that looked like a supply closet. It was much like his office at the university where he had taught anatomy to medical students — a common job for palaeontologists in lean times, he'd told her. Both the office and the van smelled of Murphy's soap. Not only that, the coffin in the back made her edgy. Did anyone really care now, besides the team? If Miguasha was like an image in time to be developed, she wondered what they would discover in the relic they were transporting. A private plane would pick them up at the small airport in Gaspé and they would deliver the body, assuming there was a body, to the coroner's office in Montreal. A mix of rain and snow fell like heavy sheets against the windows. The news from the radio was not much better.

Another communiqué came out, from the Liberation cell holding James Cross. The kidnappers declared that they were suspending the death sentence against James Cross, but they would not release him until their demands were met. He would be executed if the police found them and tried to intervene. They demanded $100,000 and the release of a number of political prisoners.

If her parents had been alive they'd be covering this one. There would be debates around the table and lectures on the history of Québec, "depending of course, on who was telling it," Robert would say. Gillian shut the radio off.

She turned to the window and stared out to the rough seacoast. The highway bordered a pastoral landscape dotted with farms, adorned with historic Québeçoise homes, permeated with tradition. Driving along the serene, slumbering countryside to the airport, Gillian felt it hard to reconcile what her eyes took in with the violent events unfolding elsewhere in the province.

"You're not still brooding?" Michel switched the radio back on.

"A trip back to Montreal is not exactly in my best interest right now."

She lay back in her seat and watched the sky empty out snow, rain, hail, and then more wet snow.

In the hour that followed in the small-engine plane, Michel talked most of the time with the pilot, who described himself as a fellow rock smasher. They were both full of energy and passionate about putting together another fossil expedition to the Arctic. On a normal day, if Gillian hadn't been so caught up in her own turmoil, she would have joined in and even offered to help with the plans.

By the time they landed at the private airstrip just outside of Montreal, the sun's rays pierced through the overcast sky that had followed them so far. As Gillian headed towards the entrance of the terminal she caught the front page of the newspaper – her sister's face was not easy to ignore. Glancing back at Michel she grabbed a copy, knowing it would be pointless to try and hide it.

"I've already read it," he told her as they climbed into another van and waited for the coffin to be transferred with their bags. "Early edition."

◉

"She likely died at about age forty, between 1820 and 1840. The bones reveal a woman somewhere in her forties, five-feet one-inch. Short and muscular, she suffered a range of health problems, from rickets to bad sinuses and bad teeth." The forensic anthropologist walked around the room, holding a partial bone from the woman's hand structure. "Her developed muscles might point to a labourer of some sort, or maybe a domestic servant? That could help explain her plain, and later forgotten, burial."

They were standing at a metal table in the coroner's lab, where the bones were neatly laid out in a skeletal formation. All the layers of human form were gone. Karin had told Gillian once that human dissection was not as stressful as she had imagined it would be. After a few weeks of dissecting, she had developed a cocky self-confidence about the whole experience and talked about cadavers as if they were her dolls.

Gillian felt restless and checked her watch. Barely forty-eight hours before, she had been sitting on a granite ledge, basking in a brief moment of contentment.

"The skull indicates a small face with a receding chin and a puckered mouth with only seven teeth. Patterns of wear suggest a high-starch diet, maybe from routine meals of local corn or wheat." This time the museum sculptor spoke while holding the skull Hamlet-style, to describe what she felt the face looked like. Her manner was like that of a woman who had just come from dissecting a table full of exotic species. "She's really a live person to me," she informed them. "I can see her." Overly confident, her hands moved quickly, her eyes twitched as she continually rolled her tongue around the insides of her mouth. The woman stopped in front of Gillian and offered the skull to her.

No – she shook her head then stepped back from the table.

The coroner continued on about the facing, cribbing techniques from two of the police forensic investigators, in hopes of creating features from the skull mold. "I'll fill in what the bones can't tell; the ears, eyelids, and hair will be based on best guesses; nose will be open to interpretation. With forty years of hard life, I can add crow's feet and lines to her face. Beyond that, we mix science and art to illustrate the personality I feel in the bones. My job is to let the bones speak."

What kind of invented history would she come up with? Would they give her a new name as well? Naming was something everyone seemed to take for granted. It was a bit late for that wasn't it? Eventually the simulated, reconstructed face would be exhibited at the museum in Québec City. The real bones would go to a cemetery in the Gaspé. A final resting place – Michel had insisted on that. At first he was the only member of the team who seemed to carry some sense of respect for the coffin. Then the others, realizing their own self-interest in the find, came up with the inscription for the gravestone: *Remains of a person known but to God – may she rest in peace.*

Another funeral. Of course it would be different than her parents'. It was as if someone had come during the night while she was sleeping and drained her of every ounce of life and when she woke up she wasn't sure she was still alive. She had to keep telling herself to breathe. It was Sophie who'd kept them moving through the motions of what to wear, what to do at the service, even how to avoid the press. Looking back for the first time, she saw the disconnectedness and now, the events of that day were being pulled together before her. The image of two coffins lowered into the ground made her feel faint. She'd wanted to scream that summer morning as she stood with her sisters in front of the gravesite. While she restrained herself, her body ached. Maude cried – Karin dabbed tears in her own sophisticated way.

Gillian felt a sudden chill in the lab and tried to think of a way to be excused from the group.

Michel came into the room looking distraught and spoke directly into her ear. "Come with me," he guided her gently, "we need to get to the hospital."

She bit the inside of her cheek and looked around the room. The faces of the students, the museum sculptor, the forensic anthropologist, were all fixed towards the table.

Michel moved her to the door. "Let's assume it's not too serious."

He was lying, she knew that much.

They drove through the city with only the heater in the van rattling for sound. An accident just before the tunnel caused him to grab her arm as he braked. She had never noticed the scars on his hands. She said nothing. Instead, her hand strayed across his and lingered as they followed the traffic, inching their way through police and ambulance trucks to the hospital.

"Room 510. She's just been moved out of ICU." A Jamaican nurse scanned the patient list. "Don't worry, she'll get through this, although I'm not sure your younger sister was assured of that. She left an hour ago. Just ran out of the hospital."

After a few wrong turns, they found Karin lying in a dingy room, plugged with tubes attached to a machine. Gillian was momentarily taken back to the table with the bones of the eighteenth-century woman.

yuri rousseau

1. You are being sued for telling a pregnant woman she needs to be tested for syphilis – TR

PS: the recruitment for more doctors ends soon.

2. Please call Sophie Frachette; family friend of Karin Digby.

He read the two messages left at the ward desk, signed himself out for forty-eight hours, and headed towards the doctor's lounge to remove his scrubs. The subtle wording in the first message didn't fail to remind him that his brother held the key to his work in this hospital. That note promptly hit the trash by the locker. As he undressed, he wondered what the photographer wanted. What else could be done? The medical resident Karin Digby would survive her personal trauma. He recommended she take a leave of absence.

What he needed was a shower, a few quiet hours, and time away from sick bodies. As he walked through the emergency exit doors onto the streets of Montreal, fresh night air welcomed him. The temperature had dropped several degrees. Snow was imminent. Before crossing the intersection, he picked up a copy of *La Press* from a corner newsstand.

PIERRE LAPORTE EST MORT!

The death of Pierre Laporte is the most tragic event of this October crisis.

According to sources, shortly before his death, Laporte was extremely restless, very depressed, and weak from loss of blood as a result of his attempt the day before to escape. He became violent and when one of his captors seized him, twisting hard on the collar of his sweater, in doing so he strangled the Minister with the chain he was wearing around his neck. By the time the man let go, Laporte was dead.

He tucked the newspaper under his arm, looked up and noticed an army truck parked on the corner. He crossed the street and saw another army jeep idling several yards from the door of the medical residency. Two soldiers, armed most likely, sat solemnly; positioned, expectant. Waiting for what? He walked several blocks towards the entrance to his own apartment block and noticed the doorman was absent this evening. He unlocked the outside door himself and went up the elevator to the twelfth floor apartment; a small corner stop-over, simply furnished – thick, brown-leather sofa, a comfortable queen-size bed, and several oil paintings he'd impulsively bought one weekend in Québec City. Apart from the housekeeper, who filled the fridge and cupboards with the kinds of food and wine he preferred and kept the place in order, he was usually alone. Tonight was no different than any other – flip the lights, adjust the dimmer, click the answering machine, and turn the television on.

"This is Sophie Frachette. I'm calling because I need to speak with you about Karen Digby and her sisters. It's urgent that we meet."

A parade of photos flashed across the television screen: Pierre Trudeau, René Lévesque, Robert Bourassa, a list of photos naming the suspects, and then images of men and women, some known others not, the army, police and jail halls of Montreal and Québec City. Journalists and camera crews seemed to be everywhere. Groups of activists were shouting as the camera followed them through the halls of government buildings. Within the last forty-eight hours, hundreds had been arrested – community workers, union organizers, singers, artists, poets, students, and even journalists. The tension depicted on the TV screen was palpable.

Abruptly, the camera caught the image of Maude Digby. He would have recognized that face in any crowd – that unique grace and presence stirred him even more than the last time they were together. Only now there was anguish – her warm green eyes were clouded in distress. Reporters followed, making any effort to get her to speak. She remained calm, stoic, and never opened her mouth. An older woman, who seemed to be working hard at making attempts to speak, followed her. No one was listening. It was the Anglophone they wanted. Why was she there? What sort of surveillance tactic could the police believe they had with someone like this, or was she being used because of her deceased parents and their journalistic connections? He stared at the screen. These kinds of uprisings he had witnessed in other countries. Hunger, language, religion, and politics; any one of these ingredients held enough potential to ignite a revolt. The reporter then read from the note left at the radio station, along with a map of the spot where Pierre Laporte's body could be found.

The arrogance of the federal government and of its hireling, Bourassa, has forced the FLQ to act. Pierre Laporte, Minister of Unemployment and Assimilation, was executed at 6:18 this evening. We shall overcome.

It would not take long before those in power would exploit these events. The next move of the FLQ members would not be easy to pin down. The manifesto was read again with details of the demands from the group underscored. How far could they go and how much did the Canadian government really understand about whom they were dealing with? Where was the link behind this group? There had to be a connection elsewhere, in order to keep them organized. In all these questions, he pushed aside the fact that the face of Maude Digby was more predominant in his mind than the potential violence that threatened the province.

He had met her twice. The first time in Murray Bay while he was stealing time at a music festival where his youngest brother Philippe was performing. It was late August and this was the sort of diversion he embraced after several months of hellish emergency medical relief in Laos. At thirty-four, he'd already acquired a long experience of war and disaster. His medical career so far had been spent doing short stints in Lebanon, Algeria, Israel, and Africa. His time in Québec was a mere scout hunt; he was hoping to lure other physicians to the battle zones. Although his roots were in France, he rarely took time to linger there. His early years of education were spent in Montreal at the insistence of his father, who felt the necessity of educating his sons in private institutes run by the Jesuits, in spite of the fact that his own wife was Jewish. Then it was off to Harvard medical school, following in the footsteps of his older brother Theo, who promptly returned to Montreal to practice. Yuri chose Paris for a short séjour, and then hit the war zones with Médicins sans Frontières; a new organization committed to medical relief. To their father's dismay and their mother's delight, none of their three sons followed the path of business. Only Philippe, the youngest, chose to make his home in Paris. That night, he was the only reason Yuri was in Murray Bay. The concert was billed as the last of the season and the seats were filled with anxious patrons, looking to evade the reality of the long, dark winter with one final taste of a summer pleasure.

"Are they taken?" a voice whispered. Dark eyes and a pensive face, mumbled a curt thanks, and he rose to let two women pass – Karin Digby, a resident from the hospital, and the younger woman he concluded must be her sister.

Theo had remarked not only on the abundant red hair but on the impact her internship as a music therapist was having at the hospital. "Our new ward healer, good with patients, especially the children."

While Yuri had never seen Maude Digby before this night, he knew more about the rest of the family, from a distance. Elle Digby had approached the medical organization several times, looking to do some coverage. Although the group appreciated the interest at certain times, Yuri felt allowing her inside to write a story could jeopardize their efforts to remain neutral. They didn't need that kind of attention.

A hush settled with a quiet applause from the audience, as the musicians walked onto the raised platform. Philippe emerged like a modest schoolboy. His days were full of scheduled concerts; he regularly appeared in the major venues of Europe and US, as a popular pianist for summer festivals, and with more invitations than his group could ever expect to fulfill. The brothers' eyes met before he took his place at the grand piano. Two other members, both male, formed the trio – Mario, a violinist from New York, and Radik, a cellist and schoolmate of Philippe's from Paris. The musicians sat down, arranged the sheet music, and tuned their instruments. Then, like true performers, they attacked in unison the opening movement. By the fourth bar of Debussy's *La Mer,* they had the minds and ears of their audience – everyone except Yuri. He was restless, unable to connect. How long could the body go without sleep?

After the concert, a not-so-refined, middle-aged board member for the festival stood to address those still seated. Like an over-anxious volunteer, he began his appeal with pictures of children with gaunt legs and enlarged abdomens; effects of the acute form of Tyrosinemia. He introduced a couple whose child had died from the disease. The story of Miriam, who'd fought since the age of three to live, clearly moved patrons to open their cheque books and donate. The audience then rose to seek out the free refreshments. Yuri rose to join them. Karin followed. They left Maude, who sat and listened intently.

"How perfectly untimely to make an appeal for money after that hour of music," Karin said reaching for a glass of white wine. "On top of it, another lecture."

They were standing under the gazebo, surrounded by pines, and looking towards the historical setting of the hills and the river, which seemed to flow together as much in harmony as the music they had experienced. He sipped his wine and watched as the young intern beside him bit her lip and then tossed back her drink.

"Isn't it odd," she said, taking a small mirror out of her handbag, "that we're here in this quiet little nook of a place, taking in a night of culture, with a War Measures act imposed on the province? Eerie, don't you think?"

"What's eerie?" Maude appeared behind them.

"I was telling Dr. Rousseau that it seems a bit strange that we've sat here in peace and isolation enjoying a concert, while in the midst of a political uprising."

"I'm still revelling in the music. By any chance do you know – wait a minute – are you related to that awesome pianist?" Maude moved towards Yuri and shook his hand.

"My brother."

"He's exceptional. I'm Maude, Karin's sister." She stared directly at him.

He remembered her hands, the slender gentleness of long fingers.

"Do you play anything as well as your brother?" she wanted to know.

"Soccer," he jested.

Her eyes brightened. "I'm talking about music."

He didn't tell her that he could have easily joined his brother's group as a violinist. That would reveal a world that she would readily enter.

"I heard you are adding new wonders to the work of medicine." He sipped his wine and stared back at her over the lip of his glass.

"I've had a long day," Karin interjected, turning to her sister. "I think we should leave." It was pointless.

"Go ahead," Maude said as she dug for her keys, then turned them over to her sister. "I don't mind walking home."

Maude and Yuri spent the next hour talking about music.

He remembered the details of that hour because it had been some time since he had enjoyed a conversation with a woman. She was passionate – not overtly opinionated like her sister. Afterwards, there having been no cues from either of them to follow up, they simply parted.

He made a pot of coffee and thought about their second meeting, several days ago. He had just returned from a weekend in the Eastern Townships with his family; a gathering to celebrate his father's eightieth birthday. What should have been a time of renewed relationships and leisurely meals had turned instead to heated debates and harsh words. Like his parents, Yuri had never been much interested in the politics of Québec. Their roots remained in France. His grandfather and father had made their money in textile mills, in Europe, the United States, New England, and the Carolinas. There had been some problems in the past with the New England mills; incidents that arose to create division amongst the English and French but they had always managed to remain negotiable and out of the political storms, as far as the Rousseaus were concerned.

Theo had been the one most involved with the political uprisings in Québec and had strong opinions about the separatist movement. The past weekend, he had been angered by Trudeau's justification of the War Measures act and the raids taking place across the province. Trudeau's comments about bleeding hearts, those who don't like to see people with helmets and guns, and how far he would go to keep law and order – all that and more, had infuriated his brother. Yuri and Theo had argued about the language issues, the summons of 6,000 soldiers to be deployed across the province, and the politicians who condemned the actions of the government. The worst, according to his brother, was the censorship on the university campuses. Only the weather had been calm that weekend. He had returned to his apartment in Montreal, feeling the weight of a relentless cloud over him. He could do nothing to fix Québec, but how about Maude Digby? When he heard his brother's voice on the answering machine, he'd been tempted to turn it off immediately.

"There's been a shooting in one of the cafés downtown," Theo's message said. "I've freed up the operating theatres and we are working on trying to assemble a disaster team. We need you in there."

His thoughts quickly turned to the number of anaesthesiologists and surgeons available as he quickly found his way over to the hospital emergency entrance.

Theo was busy directing chaos. "Before you go anywhere, I want to fill you in on several things," he started.

Yuri listened, at the same time noting the figure of a young woman lying on a bed in the corridor. He moved slowly, taking note of his brother's instructions while disturbed by the face covered with the oxygen mask – Karin Digby.

"They've notified the sisters. One is out somewhere in the Gaspé, the other driving from Québec City. That's if she can get through the convoy of army trucks."

The nurse standing beside Karin was clearly tired and making every effort to provide some comfort to her patient. Yuri read the notes.

"I want to be called when the sister, Maude Digby, arrives," he said, making every effort to remain calm.

karin

When she woke, her mouth was dry and foul, her head burned. The room was cold and sterile, and for a moment, Karin could not remember why she was lying in the hospital bed. She tried sitting up. Dizzy, her head heavy and spinning, her body limp, she lay back once, then forced herself up a second time, and felt certain she was going to vomit – but nothing.

The television blared from the ceiling. A nurse in a wrinkled uniform sat, eyes glued to the face of a local broadcaster Karin recognized from Montreal:

Laporte is a martyr. His death must not become a pointless tragedy. We must make it a milestone in the struggle for Canadian unity.

The following is an update of a letter sent to this station on the well being of kidnapped British Consul James Cross:

'I want to assure anyone who might be interested that I'm still alive and well. The FLQ assures me that I am a political prisoner and that I will be treated as such until the authorities agree to release all the FLQ activists now in jail.'

It wasn't over yet, this nightmare with the army and the FLQ descending on their lives. How far could it go? When would it end?

The door opened with Gillian balancing a breakfast tray and newspaper. She rolled the bed tray around and set a food offering in front of her. The smell of eggs caused the nausea to rise to Karin's throat and immediately she lay back down and pushed the tray to the end of the bed.

"So you're awake. Welcome back to the real world," said Gillian in a none-too-sympathetic tone.

The pain in Karin's head and neck pierced down her body. The room was too bright for her and her sister's cream shirt and grey pants seemed to shimmer in the excess light.

"What happened?"

"Think about this. Pills, doused with booze. Sophie found you passed out in the tub. Honestly Karin, what the hell were you doing?"

Was that concern in Gillian's voice? It must be the pills. She had nothing to say. Let them think the worst. She felt old and finished and she wasn't even thirty.

"Maude got here before I did," Gillian continued. "Drove in, drove out. It was all a little too much for her. Seeing you, stuck with tubes, and me wailing like a baby."

"You wailing?"

Gillian got up from the mute-green leather armchair and sat on the edge of the bed. "I know it couldn't possibly occur to you that seeing your helpless state might spin both of us into a frenzy?"

Had she been out that long? What had she missed? What was Gillian saying?

A stream of phrases poured out; only some made sense; a corpse belonging to no one; the hellish kind of a life that no one meant to be in; how she never cared about anyone really; never connected with her parents because they weren't really her parents; how Karin could easily please everyone and Maude could when she wanted, but why she didn't give a damn about anyone and now there she was in the papers, exposing them to the whole world.

"I've always believed that nothing could be salvaged by knowing things about your past, now I know it's absolutely true. Like knowing more about these kinds of mothers." Gillian threw the newspaper out onto the bed.

There were pictures and details written about families and histories and names they recognized and some they'd never heard of but were obviously supposed to have. Karin was searching for the one thing that mattered: her own name. It wasn't there and neither was Gillian's. At least they hadn't been dragged into it. The way things were now, they could let Maude get through it on her own if they wanted – it was her mess wasn't it?

Karin watched her sister grab her duffle bag and empty a paper bag with shells on the bed. Gillian's pockets usually bulged with whatever washed up on the beach and she had never let any form of crustacea pass unnoticed. She drove her family crazy until one day she quit trying to explain what their purpose might be. They all noticed the silence but no one tried to persuade her to continue or asked why she had stopped trying to enlighten them on the primitive functions of life forms from the water. But that seemed like another lifetime; Gillian might have been nine or ten. Now she stood there as if she was the child, shrouded in that cloud of innocence, looking into a tide pool.

"Take the Argonauta, a delicate shell," and she held it cautiously in the palm of her hand. "Because it happens to be one of those rare creatures from the beach world, which are not fastened to their shells but are intended only to be a cradle for the female's eggs and the neat thing is that when those eggs are ready to be released, the mother is forced out. She actually leaves the shell and starts another life or, as with some of them, goes off to shallow sands and dies.

Totally natural." She placed the shell in her sister's hand. "I suppose that's one way to consider the strange behaviour of mothers."

As Karin turned the shell over several times, she liked the feel of the fluted shape, and tried to make a connection.

"It makes me think about the woman who came into the hospital emergency with a rare ectopic pregnancy, in which the foetus had developed outside her uterus," she said. "She was taken to surgery for an emergency caesarean delivery where they soon realized the baby was not in the place it was supposed to be. The uterus did not contain the foetus. The surgeon then explored the mother's abdominal cavity and felt the feet."

"An aberration of nature," the head of obstetrics had said. "If you can imagine this, the head was near the stomach and the baby was seated near the uterus. It was an exceptional case. Babies rarely survive this unusual form of pregnancy but in this case the five-pound, thirteen-ounce baby boy was doing fine. It probably helped the mother that the placenta was attached to the base of the uterus; outside the uterus but on the base. And because it was attached to it, it helped the vascular circulation of the uterus, enabling the placenta to develop normally. Therefore the baby was nourished and continued to grow normally in the abdominal cavity."

The surgeon's description about the birth was foreign to her at the time. Karin placed the shell on her food tray.

"Yes, I guess that is one way to look at it."

Gillian picked it up, walked over to the window, and held the shell in the light. She continued her monologue on the idiosyncrasies of motherhood and the meaning of it and what children could not expect of them anyway.

It was a strange sight. Outlandish in a way, that Gillian who had fought with her mother her entire life, would be standing so vulnerable. Karin felt as if there was some sort of communication being passed between them and for the first time ever, she could sense that her middle sister was in more pain than she was. Funny how she'd never caught onto that before. Ever. It was pain that her sister was grappling with, not just anger. She never expected this.

"One way to look at what?" A voice came from the doorway.

"It's good to see you together." Sophie pulled her gloves off with her mouth, one finger at a time, then unbuttoned her black wool coat, heaved a sigh and grabbed a piece of bacon off of the breakfast tray, trying to be delicate as it went into her mouth.

Now it is going to be a conference, Karin thought as she slumped down between the sheets.

"One way to look at what?" Sophie asked a second time.

"Motherhood."

"Maybe," Sophie said, "maybe there were things in life you thought you didn't know you needed until you saw them washed up there waiting at your feet, like for instance, the shell Gillian's holding right now."

Sophie was fond of saying things like that. "When you come from a past where you've seen just about everything," she'd say, "you get on with the ebb and flow of it."

So what gave her the right now to expound on the merits of motherhood? At this moment, Karin wished she smoked. It was the inhaling and exhaling part of it that seemed to be the thing she could use right now.

"We need mothers, or at least we believe we do, as we are fearful creatures and we depend on that mother to calm all that disturbs us. In your case, you girls were given a mother; she was full of love but she was not perfect, as you desired her to be. Who can accept that there are in relationships – these sorts of limitations? Naturally you have to accept and expect those things. It is not all mutually exclusive either. And you are ready because you are old enough. Well, basically you have no choice."

Gillian turned pale.

"I'm not saying anything new here but you can both find something in this. Learn from it," Sophie continued. "And by the way, I knew your mother very well."

"And we didn't?" Gillian was furious.

"I didn't say that. What I'm saying is you didn't know her as a woman, you knew her as your mother."

"I knew about the pills and the psychiatrist."

"A sidebar," Sophie dismissed.

Karin couldn't stand it any longer. Sophie was not going to let up.

"Look, it doesn't matter now, does it? I no longer want to lie here and try to explain our mother's behaviour. And I'm tired of fighting about it."

"We'll get you out of here then, as soon as Rousseau signs you out and then I'll take you home," Sophie said, very calmly.

"I don't need him to get out of here and I'm not going back to Westmount."

"He'll have to sign your release. You did yourself in – or have you forgotten that?"

"It was a bad mix and that's what it was and no one's sticking me with anything else."

She was getting stronger by the minute, like a plant that needed water. Something was giving her energy and hope and purpose. Whatever madness had taken over her seemed to have gone, or to have been replaced with a different one. She felt her mind emptying.

"No one recovers that quickly." Sophie leaned over and put her hand on Karin's shoulder. "You need the time even if it's only for rest."

"I've got to get dressed. Get my clothes out of that closet will you, Gillian?" She pointed across the room. "They must be in there. I'm at your mercy."

Gillian opened the door and found a small leather satchel, which she recognized right away as having belonged to their mother.

"I'll help with arrangements to get out and drop you somewhere but you're not following me anywhere," Gillian insisted. "Especially not back to the Gaspé and especially not to the burial."

"What burial?"

"The unknown woman. We've decided to give her a proper ceremony. I'm meeting the team there as soon as I can get out of this place. Michel is flying us out of Montreal."

"And I'm going with you," Karin said as she pulled her pants on and threw off the hospital gown. "I hope he doesn't mind having an extra passenger."

Sophie was ignored. She shuffled through her purse and pulled out a lipstick holder, went over to the bathroom, wiped the mirror with a paper towel, then leaned over the sink and traced red strokes across her lips. Karin looked back at her while straightening the wrinkles in her turtleneck sweater. For the moment, the floor seemed very far away – it went with the tightness in her chest and a fear she was going to faint or fall. There was an odd sensation and then it was gone. She uncovered the lunch tray and stuffed two pieces of unbuttered bread into her mouth. As she did this, her eyes reluctantly met Sophie's.

"I know what you're thinking so don't bother to say it," Karin said. "Don't even bother."

"It's just that you need to realize some things."

"If you mention anything else about what it is we need to realize, I'll throw something."

Karin brushed by Sophie, went towards a small wooden end table where the phone sat, dialled the ward desk and asked the clerk to page Dr. Jenny Bird.

"If we take you with us," Gillian said, "you have to promise me that you won't discuss the shell thing when Michel's around." She wandered around the room, then turned back to the food tray, picked up the shell and stuffed it into her bag. "I've spilled my guts to you and there's no way I want him knowing a thing about this conversation. A marine biologist would find all that somewhat pathetic."

"Is that it? Is that all I have to do; keep my mouth shut about shells and mothers?"

"The newspaper," Sophie interjected. "Can I ask what you are both going to do about that at least?"

The phone rang. Karin lifted the receiver. "Jenny, it's me. Of course, I'm ok. I have to get out of the hospital. It's urgent. There's a funeral I need to get to. Can you find out who covers for Rousseau and get them to release me?" She slammed down the receiver, picked the newspaper off the bed and tried very hard to be objective. What could they possibly do about it? Call Maude? Not now, not with Gillian and Sophie standing there. She had the energy for this trip away from Montreal and out to the cold, ghastly peninsula at the end of nowhere but not for the complicated unravelling of whatever their sister had unearthed her way into. Did they want to know right now?

"Gillian?" Karin screwed up her face with disgust.

Gillian shook her head. "I've got a funeral to attend. I can't wait for you to be discharged." Then she turned to gather her bag and the shell and left the room without her sister.

maude

the trouble with adoptees finding their birth parents, Maude told herself, as the landscape passed in a kaleidoscopic blur, is that the abandoned baby has grown up. The past that might have been your own no longer belongs to you. You have to rely on others to tell you what might have been. But if you couldn't bring it to the present, then what was the point of it?

Today, everyone was stunned by Pierre Laporte's murder. Even René Lévesque had distanced himself from the radical movement. There were rumours that the FLQ had enough machine guns and dynamite to launch an urban guerrilla war.

"The worst of it," Trudeau announced," is that the terrorists are children of people we know."

Like mine? How many of those bombs had they constructed? How does someone like Finn Cavanagh, her biological father, become so passionately involved in another country's problems? Robert and Finn, both from elsewhere, yet implicated in the affairs of a country not their own.

With hands stuck to the wheel, she leaned forward, straining to keep her eyes fixed on the highway past the cape, the Montmorency Falls tumbling white and foamy between the firs, beyond the orchards of l'Isle d'Orleans. Twenty-four hours earlier, she had inched her way through traffic on the highway lined with convoys of dark-green army trucks to Montreal, only to end up before the hopeless state of her sister.

As she drove taking in the morning air, she could not stop thinking how Yuri had caught her elbow as she fainted at the first sight of Karin. Embarrassed, she let him gently lower her to the floor, then bent her face to her knees and wrapped her arms over her head.

"Try to breathe."

She raised her head as he awkwardly placed his arms under hers. She let him help her up.

"I'm going to be sick..." She pushed him away with the palms of her hands and leaned against the wall for support. She coughed and gagged.

"Sit here," he said, pushing a chair under her knees. She shivered. He grabbed a blanket from a metal cabinet and wrapped it around her shoulders. It took a few minutes for the shock to subside.

He stood quietly beside her. "Your sister will be out for a while, perhaps you should eat something."

"I need air," she said and let the blanket slide to the floor.

"I'll walk with you."

"No, please, I'm fine, I want to be alone." She looked at his face and stood silent. Then, as if lightning had struck, she picked up her coat and purse and bolted out through the hospital doors.

Now, she needed the sea and the potent seclusion of Murray Bay. But the grey-shrouded coastline only seemed to stoke the chaos in her mind. She turned from the highway into the closed shutters on the summer homes – a usual sign that the city dwellers were headed to Montreal. There was barely a sign of any community life. Some of the flat-bottomed boats were beached. A couple of fishing vessels were moored in the deeper water. Driving the dirt roads through the Bay, its signature stone farmhouses, and windmills scrolling by gave her comfort. She passed the golf course, a main attraction for as long as her grandparents' family had summered here, before the Second World War. Then came the American invasion as they called it – families from New England moving north. Robert would go on about the endless hours spent on the golf course, the tennis tournaments, and the afternoons at the Manoir swimming pool with the Ramonelli Orchestra in the background. She remembered her first time as a child listening to Prokofiev's *Peter and the Wolf* and *The Ugly Duckling* at the classical music festival. It was during those summers that her decision to become a music therapist had transpired so naturally, just as Gillian vowed never to leave working the ocean shores, and for some strange reason, Karin made up her mind to pursue medicine.

Amidst the roadside apple and strawberry farmers, and the plein air artists dragging their canvases down to the water's edge, she could see how Anna belonged. How many summers had they been there at the same time – the artist and the activist? Turning onto Rue St. Pierre towards the old cottage, the memory of the photograph of Anna, Finn, and Elle on the dresser caused her to brake. The real story about their past had been right before her.

She spotted the mallard curled on the steps, as calm as that first day when she'd moved in. This time she observed the bird with more interest. Was it a stray or did it just prefer the shelter of a porch to the wind and water?

But there was someone else waiting. Twenty-some years can add changes to a face but as she walked the path to the front door, she recognized him from the picture at Anna's house. His eyes did not blink. She matched his gaze. It was a looking glass experience. If fathers are intended to be mirrors, reflecting back an image of one's self, there was no doubt she felt this one to be distorted. He had a boyish look with marine-blue eyes set deeply into his face, and hair, too long, gave his face a round look, at odds with his wishbone cheeks. He was slim. His hands were small and his arms dangled at his sides as if they were numb. When he finally spoke, she realized she'd been holding her breath.

"Judging by your face, you know who I am. Now let me look at you." He wasn't the least bit uneasy. "Well, you've certainly opened up a can of worms haven't you?"

She was not prepared for this awkward conversation. She noted his clothing; well dressed, reminding her of Robert, especially the loafers. She stood fixated on a pair of shoes, figuring out what to say next.

"If it means anything, I put up a fight to keep you for Anna's sake but there wasn't a chance for us to work it out – they wouldn't allow it. We would have raised you and loved you." And then he choked. His eyes were glassy. He took a lighter and pack of cigarettes out of his coat pocket.

She stood frozen, with her hands pressed tight to her purse, hearing the words of the man standing in front of her though she wasn't sure she could have repeated them. In her mind, she moved from the loafers to an image of the sea horse laying her eggs in the male's pouch, then carrying them to term and bearing the babies. Would life be different if males had to figure what to do with babies?

"You look healthy and beautiful."

His gestures were awkward. She could tell that he wanted to touch her but she stepped back.

"Look, I know this seems all bad." His accent was heavier now.

"Which mother are you talking about?" Maude steeled herself, drilled to stay calm.

"What are you saying?" He backed away.

"I'm asking you which one – Anna or Elle? Which one didn't you have a chance with?" Her mouth went dry, and she bit her bottom lip.

"Anna of course."

She felt steady now, unnerving and determined to let him know that she wasn't going to unravel for him. He could try to cover things up for whatever reason they all had agreed upon in the past but all that was over. Stuck like a burr in her mind was the room where she'd slept at Anna's and the photograph of the three of them.

"Look." He stepped towards her, reaching out to put his hand on her shoulder. "I'm not sure what you're trying to say."

"Just tell the truth. I've figured it all out anyway. All you have to do is tell me I'm right. I know everything and now all I want from you is to say it's true. You knew them both."

"I'm not sure which version of the past you seem to think you know. You can dig the wells of history and take the version that fits your need but you really don't know because you weren't there." He lit another cigarette. "So are we going to just stand here in the cold or will you invite me in?"

She did not want to invite him into the house for tea or coffee or anything else he might drink. As she fumbled through her purse for door keys, rolling excuses in her head, she heard a car slowly driving into the gravel road. As the vehicle parked across the street, they both turned at the same time. Most likely the FLQ had followed him – of course they would. She hoped it might even be the police. She was ready now to talk, to tell them everything this time and let them work out the rest. But when the car door opened, she was startled to see Yuri. He walked across the grass towards them both. Outwardly cool, inside she trembled.

Passing Finn with a nod, Yuri leaned toward her and brushed his lips against her cheek. "I thought I should check on you."

"I'm ok," she lied.

"You have company."

Her eyes met his. There was a newspaper rolled under his arm but he made no attempt to show it to her. Instead, he moved towards Finn, extended his hand, and introduced himself.

Then Finn spoke. "Well, I think we can take this up again – most likely you've had enough for one day." Nodding at them both, he turned towards his own vehicle, parked across the street.

"I'll be in touch," raising his hand yet not looking back as he left.

She wondered if she would ever see him again. The lights from his car awakened her to the silence of steady snow and darkness as it descended over them.

"Shall we go in?" Yuri suggested.

It took a minute or two for the strangeness to leave her but she did not want to be alone. In silence, they entered the house to the smell of polish and the hum of the heating system, finally turned on by the housekeeper. She placed her keys on the oak sideboard and removed her coat.

"I'll take yours."

The scent of wet wool filled her nostrils. He placed the newspaper carefully beside her keys. He moved past the wide entrance and went into the kitchen. He was calm, with an air of confidence that made her want to lean against him. Instead, she rummaged through the cupboards to offer him something: a brandy, wine – what would he drink?

"Do you suppose he's still involved with the movement?" she asked.

He appeared around the corner of the kitchen and leaned against the doorframe. "There's a possibility that things are not as they seem but before you try to figure that out, you must eat," and then proceeded to open the fridge.

"I don't cook much," she yawned, "so you won't find enough of anything in there unless the housekeeper has stocked it."

She moved towards the wide oak table that divided the cooking area and watched him pull from a sparsely stocked fridge – eggs, cheese, tomatoes, leftover ham and milk. From the rack that hung over the wooden island in the centre, he grabbed a pan. Meticulously, he chopped and mixed the ingredients as if he were in his operating room. It struck her that while she was in a state of absolute confusion, she was about to eat the tastiest omelette of her life. Like the last mother she had worked with. She had just experienced the complex delivery of a baby boy with multiple health problems, yet when she went to visit her, the room was full of warmth and sunshine, covering any shade of trauma.

"Tell me about your family," she said.

"Well, you've already met two brothers." He licked his fingers and put the omelette before her. "That's it, three males essentially grown up, dispersed."

She felt strangely connected to his brothers. Theo Rousseau, Chief of Staff at the hospital, and in spite of the rumours of a shady connection to the FLQ, had called her the 'new ward healer' when she started her internship as a music therapist. The night with Philippe at the music festival had brought them together for the first time.

"And your mother, how does she feel about this?"

"Well, we're not exactly tied to our mothers are we?"

He placed the food on plates and they stood at the counter eating.

"Tell me about your mother," she persisted.

"My mother's presence in my life was something I probably took for granted. She was always there and yet she had her own way of allowing us to discover life on our own."

"Like how?"

"I remember moving to a small village outside of Paris with my mother and brothers for what was supposed to be a sabbatical for her. We stayed for five carefree years, other than resisting the fact that someday we would have to move back to Paris and work as hard as our father. My mother gave us that time, I suppose, just to grow and observe. I spent all mine in the hills, dissecting insects and chasing wild birds."

"And that's how you came to choose medicine?"

"I'm not sure, I've never seen it that way."

"Unlike my sister, who goes into medicine thinking she'll please her father." She yawned again.

"Or yourself, the one who likes tracking relatives from the past." His plate was empty. He leaned over the counter to kiss her.

"Some of us have to," Maude said after his lips had pressed hers.

She left the table and walked through the hall past the sideboard table. The cover of his French newspaper glared back at her and she picked it up. Whatever the language, it read like fiction. The details in this edition were more explicit, with names and then a long history of Finn's involvement with the movement; cell groups formed in the '50s and '60s. At first, she could hardly look at the photos. Then she began to study them meticulously. She examined her face, then Anna's. She did not see the resemblance. Except for the red curls, her nose, and chin were different. What did she expect? Had Anna known all along where her baby was raised? She wondered how a woman could forgive a man who'd betrayed her.

Maude ran her hands across the image of Elle in her business suit and black beret. Elle had been full of that kind of unassuming demeanour and the thing about her was everyone always supposed that she had things together. How could she have fallen into this triangle? Finn had the *Star* reporter and the child artist captivated. Did Robert know? If he did know, why was he willing to live with it all? Maybe he'd known about Karin's father or Gillian's. The phone rang.

"I've just arrived in Montreal." It was Aunt Grace.

"I land and pick up a paper. Bloody hell. As Jefferson would say – the man who reads nothing at all is better off than the one who only reads the newspapers. I hope what I'm holding in my hand is a mistake. I leave the country for three months and come back to history being rewritten. And that woman you're with in the paper.

She's the artist I've scheduled to show for the month of November. What were you doing with her in jail, of all places?"

"It wasn't like I was in jail," said Maude, indignant now. "When I have a chance to figure it out I'll explain. Can you hold on at least till you get back to the Bay?"

"Well, it's all very interesting how they can drum up stories these days." Grace's own indignation was rising. "Lies, all lies, whatever's behind this piece. Your mother would never have been involved in anything but the truth; the real story. She did everything for that paper. She had to get to the source and she's never been appreciated enough for that. Never. No woman reporter had the guts she had. She wrote about the bombings and that janitor being killed. Now that she's gone, they want dirt about her."

"Can we wait to talk about this?"

"Why wait when it's already happened? Now we have to figure out what we are going to do about it," Grace insisted.

"I have company here," Maude said uneasily as she stared around the corner into the kitchen.

"Who?"

"I doubt you know him – Dr. Rousseau."

"Not related to the Rousseau, mentioned in the newspaper, I hope. His name is Theo Rousseau. They bring him out of the woodwork now that he's Chief of Staff at the hospital. No bloody respect for anyone."

Maude hadn't seen that name the first time but as she held the receiver between her shoulder and her ear, she turned to the middle section of the newspaper and there it was – Theo Rousseau, medical student at the time, part of the group that Finn was linked to.

"Well is he or not?"

She watched as Yuri tidied the remains of the cooking fare, carefully washing and replacing the pan and utensils back from where he had plucked them.

"I'm not sure," she lied and hung the receiver back on the wall. She was trembling now. Before she could move, he was standing in front of her.

"You've known all along about this?" she asked.

"Some of it, not everything, not yet."

"I'm being used?" She raised her voice.

"Not really," he said.

There was no courage left to confront him. He said that like her, there were things he had to know. Obviously he was aware of his own brother's involvement but he wasn't about to discuss it while she was angry. Instead, he reached for his coat and left.

The next morning, the air was crisp. She felt the wind on her face as rough ice; so cold it felt like walking into a deep freeze. The front garden looked desolate, the frozen fuchsias needed mulching and some of the plants were past ready to be uprooted. She walked down the wooded path alone, not another soul, only birds skimming over the beach. Hopefully there would be no early morning walkers who might recognize her.

"It's still a friendly community here, we look out for each other. No need to be alone." Her aunt liked to brag about her neighbours.

"I'm an adult woman who has a right to privacy," replied Maude, and now she felt the world knew more about her than she did. She thought about calling the hospital to check in on her sister but couldn't do that either. Once they read the paper, they would disown her, she was certain of that. Their lives were continually spiralling out of normalcy. How could she even be sure they'd want to see her again?

Maude arrived at the gallery and unlocked the wooden door into the front entrance. Inside was so cold that she kept her coat on until the furnace had time to heat. She headed towards the small studio in the back, to retrieve her pencils, watercolours, books, and objects she had stored in a flat drawer. It had started as an exercise during her music studies when she had been obliged to sketch a page a day. Of all the visual arts, she felt that drawing was the most analogous to music. She preferred to work with pencil drawings at this point, rather than watercolours. She was intrigued by the simple transparency of expression. She had started a series on what the hands could reveal. She'd once visited a showing of Corot's work and been taken by the image of Hagar, the Egyptian handmaiden driven out into the desert by Abraham's barren wife. Hagar was languishing in thirst when an angel pointed to a fountain of water. Maude had forgotten about it for some time until the summer before her parents died.

The gallery had been featuring paintings from a Spanish artist named Sunal Alvar. Mystical depictions of a Biblical suite - Ruth gleaning, Esther ruling, and Lot's wife with her hands poised behind her, looking back. She most likely would have looked back, Maude remembered thinking. She was good at that wasn't she?

"Oppressive stories about keeping women out," Elle said when she had found Maude sketching.

Maude wanted to capture those transforming moments. The piece she was now working on had turned into a study of hands; the hands of the child, the hand of the angel pointing to the stream, and Hagar's hands reaching for her dying child. In an effort to follow the progression of some underlying unity, Gillian had collected drawings of limbs and the stages of developing hands in humans and animals. Now Maude wished she had those images. Or that Gillian could be with her, sharing the details. What a mess. She thought of her sisters as she diligently sketched for what seemed like several hours, attempting to reconstruct Hagar's hands until she felt her efforts in vain, futile. She hadn't set out to get so involved in the exercise.

She stopped and went into the small kitchen to make coffee. As she moved through the back room, Maude noticed a crate that had arrived from Québec City. She found a hammer from the toolbox in the armoire and started to carefully pull the nails out of the wooden crate. She was physically stronger than she would ever give herself credit for. As she ripped the brown packaging off each canvas, she noticed the signature AT painted in bold letters on the back of each one.

Attached to the crate was a list that identified the pieces. *Beach Scene, Paris Beach, Beach Mornings, Afternoon at the Beach, Murray Bay,* a close-up view of figures on the beach with multi-coloured patterns of umbrellas. *Morning on the Beach* stood out more than the others; dazzled with purple water, it depicted an extremely low horizon that took almost all of the painting, and then was taken up by a subtly flecked, cloudless sky. Another painting, unnamed, displayed a wispy arabesque in the sand –'art nouveau in spirit' her aunt would mostly like say—with the emphasis on colour, laid on at times in broad, flat washes suggesting the impact of French Fauvism. Then there was *Mother and Child in a Garden,* showing a strong sense of familial bonding, surrounded by a light-glistening garden, with forms of tree and foliage.

There didn't seem to be much variety in Anna's work, Maude thought. Was it lack of imagination or just torment? The beach, the children, and trees – at least the style and tones were layered with detail and depth that drew you into the scenes leaving different impressions each time she studied them.

She began to walk around the gallery, removing the other artists' work from the panels, replacing them with some of Anna's smaller paintings. She retreated several steps to the centre, in an attempt to decide whether she might find something else in this woman's work that would draw her in. Walking backwards to get a better perspective, she caught a glimpse from a shadow of someone at the front entrance. Her throat tightened. It was already five o'clock and October's darkness had set in. She hoped the front door was still locked – she hadn't bothered with it when she entered this morning.

A knock. She hesitated and stood back from the window panel, enough to get a glimpse of the night impression.

"Don't be frightened," a male voice said.

"You followed me?" Immobilized at the door, she waited.

"Will you let me in?"

She couldn't remember opening the door. He stared but didn't speak. His eyes were dark, a slatey colour, she hadn't noticed before and she found them difficult to penetrate this time. Not at all like their first meeting where she felt she could almost hear his thoughts. Finn nervously waited. She watched him scan the room. He turned away from her and went and stood at the display panels where the paintings belonging to Anna were spread out.

"The work has steadily progressed."

"Do you like them?"

"They sell don't they? Somebody likes them obviously."

"That's not what I asked."

"I suppose she's become an old-fashioned mode of how the artist should live and behave, compared to the generation now when artists spend more time in expensive restaurants and fashionable resorts than in their studios. But she's out of touch you know, not out there enough."

"But why should she be, if she's producing as much as she does in her studio? Maybe she doesn't feel the pressure of being terribly famous and successful. Her paintings are infused with deep feeling."

"You've caught something I've missed; a woman's thing I imagine. I'm clearly out of sync – prefer the obscure, the mythological treatments. Whatever you think, she'll most likely remain the sort of painter about whom not much is known."

"Until now," Maude interjected.

"You've got a point there." He laughed. "Anna's got the press around her now, hasn't she?"

He walked to the far end of the gallery and pointed to several pieces from other artists that were hanging and said, "This is good. I don't even like sea otters, or sea urchins, whatever you call them but look at these fellows, having a great time of it on their backs." He busied himself for several minutes checking prices, lifting framed paintings off the walls, turning them over, reading bios.

"Did I happen to mention that we named you after one grand lady – Maud Gonne. Do you know anything at all about her?"

"We? Are you talking about Elle?"

"This time you've got it. That's right. Anna was too young, too baffled by it all to even come up with a name. But Elle was on to it. Fascinated with her. Maud Gonne that is. Knew everything about her life. The politics, the French lover, the Russian assignment – in fact, she wanted to write her own book about her. Surely she talked to you about that?"

"No."

"Never? Really, I'm staggered. I suppose it became difficult for her. Of course it was. Robert wasn't interested. Until later, of course, when the Troubles manifested on his turf – when it appeared things would disrupt his little world. But you, you must read about Maud Gonne. Get to know the woman and you'll understand something about your own mother. She will inspire you no doubt. Of course she had her dark side, naturally, and there were stories, lots of them – the rumours but one gets used to that. My God, she did." He was drifting back and forth between Elle and Maud Gonne; it was hard to follow him.

"I don't have a clue about this woman. I don't know anything about her. At this point, I don't seem to know much about my own mother. I mean Elle Digby, the woman who raised me. I want to know about her. Is the newspaper right?" She spoke slowly while trying hard to not to break down.

"What?" He was off now in his own production. "Yes and no. You see, I knew her and you knew her, and the newspaper thought they knew her. But really, we've each just had a glimpse haven't we?"

Was he talking about his heroine or her mother? He was emotional. Confused, she thought. He talked about the two women as if they were so familiar and linked together as close as family. Did he have any idea of the absurdity of it all?

"We wonder if we've made the right choices sometimes, like you letting me into this place." He paced back and forth, nervously. "I knew her story, a different version, no doubt than what you grew up with. She made ripples everywhere. Her frankness and directness got her places." He lit a cigarette. "Listen, it's like this in a way. Look at these paintings – some of them are very good. You get the meaning, you're impressed, then nothing. But then sometimes one of these images moves you and draws you into the scene, and you are overcome…so taken, that you want to go there, wherever it is." He took a stool and sat down. "That first night at the café in Montreal, when she came over and joined our table, so keen to get an interview, it was like the landscape changed – a bit like a painting coming to life." He inhaled and continued, "She asked the questions, I answered. Our thoughts met as naturally as our eyes. It began like that. Ideas, the movements, a friendship, we were in no hurry to go where we knew it was leading. Then just when we both felt we couldn't stand it anymore, the unforeseen happened."

"But she was married and you were already involved with Anna. Didn't any of it count?"

"What do you think? You're old enough to know the facts and digging for all this past – why not? Why shouldn't I give it to you straight? She came one night to my place, ready to make what could have been a mistake, I guess, but I couldn't do it. I surprised even myself. I wanted her, but couldn't do it, just couldn't."

The distant past was too much to take in. She went back into the kitchen and poured the cold tea into a chipped cup and swallowed hard.

He came up behind her and put his hand on her shoulder. "Please."

She moved past him back into the gallery room.

He kept talking. "Before you think the very worst of me, you should talk to Sophie."

"Sophie?"

"That's right. Talk to her, and the Rousseaus while you're at it."

"Theo Rousseau?"

"Yes, the brother of the man you are seeing."

"I'm not seeing him."

He ignored her defence. "Theo had the money; the means to do things. That's all. It cost money to keep it going. Theo was different back then. All of us were filled with ideals, dreams and, oh yes, illusions. What's that saying – illusions are dangerous people, they have no flaws?" He turned again towards Anna's paintings and picked up a rope that had been left lying with the package. He began to unravel the knot. "Even with the market in a bit of a slump, she might have done better if she'd only stayed in Paris – traveled a bit more." He sighed. "And Elle, she was naïve for a reporter. She could tell the stories but she couldn't handle the facts. People die. You lose everything in the end." He was drifting. "It's all bloody awful and the worst things come out in it. Nothing hits you like the betrayal – nothing about a man who believes in one set of ideals but gets blackmailed into denying them." He stood in front of her now. "When the old guy at McGill died, the watchman, she was shocked. So shaken up, that everything changed between us."

"Robert?" Her eyes were brimming. "Where was Robert?" *Karin would absolutely want to be dead, if she knew this.*

"No idea what the chap was up to," he replied. "In his head, I mean. Maybe Sophie can clue you in on that. Fill in some of the gaps."

"Sophie?" She repeated herself in disbelief.

"That's right." He pulled out the chair behind the purchasing counter, placed it in the middle of the room and straddled it. "I suggest you talk to her about everything. She's more than ready to have it out there. Why do you think it's in the paper now?"

"It's in the paper because the FLQ are causing everyone to be suspicious and we happened to be hauled in together because we were in the same place when they barged in and took us for questioning. It was Anna they wanted, not me."

"Anna has nothing to do with anything and the police know that already and have for years.'

"How can you say that?"

"Because I happen to know it's the truth. Look, you need to get this straight from the one person who can lay it out for you. Sophie's your source for all of it and the story in the newspaper."

"I have no reason to believe anything you say." She shut her eyes. "And why haven't you been taken in for questioning? You were the one who caused all the problems. Why are you not behind bars and why, if everyone else is innocent, are they being dragged in and the one who's the real criminal is sitting here?"

He stood up and put the chair behind the counter. Red blotches appeared on his cheeks and it took some moments before he composed himself. She opened her mouth to speak further but he held his hand up. He picked up a pen and scribbled on a piece of paper. As he handed it to her, he calmly said, "You talk to Sophie, then if ever you want to finish this conversation, here's a private number where I can be reached. And for the record, if we should ever speak again, I resent being addressed as a criminal."

He picked up his coat and walked to the door. "Pseudo cells – get her to explain that one."

gillian

temperance and Perseverance frame the majestic neo-gothic façade of Montreal's Notre Dame Basilica. The distinguished twin towers convey a certain kind of power that connects spiritual seekers with the mystical. The stained glass windows filter light through three ceiling windows, bathing the spectacle in a wondrous natural glow. In Temperance, the eastern tower, there is a carillon consisting of ten bells. Perseverance carries Le Grand Bourdon, the heaviest bell in the Western Hemisphere weighing in at 10,900 kilograms. When it tolls at Christmas, Easter, or Corpus Christi, the sound can be heard twenty kilometres away.

Normally, the oldest Catholic church in Montreal would be overtaken with tours of travelers admiring the seventeenth century architecture. Instead it was full on this October morning with dignitaries, politicians, family, and friends. Under the blue vaulted ceiling studded with thousands of twenty-four carat gold stars, sat Trudeau, Lévesque, and Bourassa, united together for the first time. Pierre Laporte had not only been a personal friend but his death had shaken the three men to their cores; this was beyond any political challenge they would ever know. No one was prepared for the brutality of the two kidnappings, let alone a murder. Lévesque called it, 'the way of the rats.'

Another bell tolled from the village of Pointe St. Pierre, situated on the outskirts of Miguasha Park. Unusually high for a graveyard and hidden amongst the rock cliffs, this was one of the better sites where the bones could be put to rest for the last time, the team agreed. The only highlight of this piece of earth was the spectacular view of the bay, a calming presence for the living. On the horizon, a liner sat either anchored or sailing; from a distance nothing was that clear. The coastal waters of the Gaspé were famously menacing and had claimed a number of shipwrecks; this landmark cemetery stood as a testament. In the depths of the bay, the lost liner from the Québec City – Liverpool run; the Empress of Ireland, lay in its own burial place.

The rest of the landscape was equally desolate. Instead of mowed lawns and trimmed trees, there was broken asphalt, barbed wire, and split fence posts. No one wanted to utter the words 'abandoned cemetery,' but it was hard to imagine anyone coming to visit the dead there. There were graves marked by rotten crosses while others, visibly weather-torn, supported broken angels. Slabs crusted with lichen, deteriorated so that names like Thomas Henry Jones, wife and son - Ireland, died of cholera; Hammond Gowen – born Boston July 1784 – departed this life 1864; and Jasper Boyd Andrews 1896-1917 – killed in action at St. Nazare, France – were barely visible.

After climbing the rocky terrain through the wicket gates at the cemetery, towards the chosen gravesite for a woman none of them knew, Gillian concluded that laying someone to rest was an enormous responsibility. The day seemed too sunny for a funeral. She carried small pots of chrysanthemum blooms from a local nursery, having tried to imagine what sort of flower might please this woman; roses, lilies or maybe lilacs – there wasn't much of a choice, considering the season. The Gaspé was always colder than the rest of the province – the surrounding landscape was more than ready for winter. Her small group stood to one side of a dug-out burial plot. She waited and wished her duffle coat was at least six inches longer. She envied Michel's mid-length fur coat, which had initially embarrassed her at the airport earlier. But now, solemnly waiting with the rest of the team for some sort of a service to begin, she longed for comfort. A red-tailed hawk shrilled, then flew over them. She scanned the sky for another; usually when they called out like that they were mating.

She checked her watch, almost three o'clock. In one hour, dusk would drain the color from the landscape and the ceremony, or whatever it was they had put together, would be over. She dug into her pockets for Kleenex and waited for a sign from the tweed-suited, long-haired minister with the red tie tucked into his jacket. Before the hike up to the gravesite, he had quietly asked if there were any hymns they would like to sing. They confessed to being only vaguely aware of songs for the dead, except for Gillian who wasn't about to share at this time the chosen music from her parents' funeral. In difficult times, Sophie had told them, the soul needs Beethoven. The sisters had been too shocked to know. Gillian had read in a pamphlet handed to her after the death of her parents, how everyone responds to personal tragedies in different ways. Grief comes in increments, it stated, and reality becomes more painful as the magnitude of the loss sets in. The pamphlet also advised that things have to get a lot worse before they get better. She had shoved that piece of information into the same bag she'd packed for Karin for the hospital.

The word had spread through the townships that there were others besides the team mounting the hill – some out of curiosity and for respect, they said. On the periphery, in a red fox fur with matching hat, Sophie stood like a distant relative with her German shepherd Jacques beside her. Very much the islander now, Gillian thought, an identity borrowed when she moved to the region with the intention of settling in with a lover from Montreal, who had never made it. At least that was the story Sophie told them. The house had been purchased and need of repairs. So with a few tools and no experience she hammered and nailed for two years until the sting of romance gone wrong left her.

When the crowd on the hill was ready, the minister gripping his Bible and trembling with cold, cleared his throat and motioned for the bagpipes. Myles, one of the team members, who called himself a dark, dour Scot from the wild Highlands, pulled a folded piece of brown paper from his pocket and began to read lines from Poe's *Valley of the Unrest.*

After several attempts to fill the pipes, the Scot performed with gusto the first of the only three hymns he knew, *Amazing Grace*.

The minister appeared to draw his courage from this and with a sudden boldness began to read the invocation. "O God our Father, who created us human beings in Your likeness, male and female, You looked at all you created and said, 'Behold, it is very good'; we rejoice and are gladdened that no one is a nobody to You, no one is a stranger to You, and no one is ever beyond Your love. Dignity is every person's birthright because every person possesses a freedom of choice, self-consciousness, thoughtful creativity, moral judgment, an intelligent mind, self-understanding, and personality. There is much more to a life than mere physical characteristics. There is spirit – the very stamp of our creation. So we witness today to the value of every human being – not the least is this unknown woman. But who is this person that our Creator and we should be mindful of? We all belong to the human family. Our sister has died. She is precious to our Father. Therefore, she is precious to us. To God we commit her keeping."

The bones sprawled on the table at the lab need a life breathed into them, Gillian told herself. Nobody had a clue about her life. The woman had been dead for two hundred years but this guy spoke like he had known her all his life. Gillian picked up the chrysanthemum blooms and placed them around the casket.

Myles continued with the funeral hymn, *Beyond the Sunset* – there were no words to accompany it, then another prayer was uttered before the wooden box was lowered into the hole. It was cold, yet the ground had not frozen enough to avoid putting the box into the grave. Michel pushed a lump of damp earth into Gillian's hand. She walked to the edge and let it sift slowly. The earth was thrown, the last shovel of dirt settled, and the silence grew. A stone engraving had been crafted and would later be placed – 'To the honour and memory of the remains of a person known but to God.'

"Shall we move on to the pub then?" Myles was the first to speak.

"Well no one has exactly prepared a reception have they?" Michel agreed. He turned to the others who were pre-occupied with shuffling hands and feet to keep warm now that the silence of the service had been broken. If the ceremony was to be significant, it needed to be commemorated with food to sanctify and seal it, Myles instructed them. Michel made an attempt to include the minister by inviting him to join the group but he politely replied that his wife and children were waiting for him for supper. Gillian motioned to Sophie to follow. Without hesitation, she led the group back down the hill towards the village, past the quay and several harbour-side houses where they were observed through the curtains of the local residents. The prospects of a rough winter were evident. Both sea and sky were now brooding grey and the beach inhospitable.

Gillian was the first to open the way into the clouds of the smoke-filled haze of *Réne's*, the first neon-lit pub they could enter. The room was a full mix of locals and Europeans hanging on past the tourist season for winter activities.

"More coming every year." Michel nudged Gillian towards the section at the back.

Sophie followed, after a short exchange with the bartender. Within several minutes, a table was cleared for the team.

"They don't mind a bit," Sophie said, directing everyone to their seats.

This would be the team's last meal together. They waited during an uneasy shuffling of chairs, coats, and scarves before sitting down. Beyond the borders of the dig, until the ceremony at the gravesite had finished, there was awkwardness. In spite of it, Gillian was grateful to be in Gaspé. Sophie could hover and direct the group, and order the food and drinks. It was at this moment, for the first time in what seemed liked a very long time, Gillian was finding new life in the familiar. She stared at the group around the table.

"Well we never imagined the dig would end putting bones to rest, but except for one or two of us, our paths may not cross again, so all the best to each of you," Michel said.

With raised glasses, they exchanged warm remarks around the table. The panoply of mussels, fries, and cod sticks was devoured as quickly as it was hastily set before them. Gillian could not eat.

"Prehistory doesn't come in neat packages," Michel had said during her interview for the summer job at Miguasha. "But in bits and pieces that must be catalogued in layers and layers that need sorting and if you dig deep enough and carefully, it is possible to pull together all kinds of stories, through the details of the past."

At the time, she had been certain she wanted to work with him for the rest of her life. That was only five months ago. Now he was off to Greenland and other parts of the planet where there were opportunities to dig. She would not let herself think about how that was going to change things for her this year. Not at this moment.

"So what happens next?" Sophie leaned over to break into her thoughts.

"Who knows?" Gillian held her glass with both hands.

"Well, we get through the long overdue trial and maybe that will be the end of this weight of the past."

"There is going to be a trial?"

"Sans doute. It is due. The roundup brought that about. Or can we say, the kidnappings and murder. Maybe this time they'll get it right."

"What do you mean?" Gillian said as Sophie edged closer.

"The inevitable – that the past catches up and finally these two are going to get what they deserve." Sophie took her glasses out of her purse, and after wiping and adjusting, reached in again, this time for a newspaper clipping.

What seemed so matter of fact for her mother's friend landed like a bomb before Gillian. "I have no idea what you are talking about. And we've seen that clipping before. That is Maude's story, she can deal with it."

"You haven't seen this one, *The FLQ's First Murder*, the one your mother wrote about – the murder of the night watchman in '63. It may be providential that she isn't here to go through this, now that Finn and Theo Rousseau, the masterminds behind the first murder and most likely the recent one, are back in the spotlight."

"In the '60s," Michel pitched in, with more food, "I recall there was a trial for that one – a battery of lawyers and prisoners. Dealt with, done with." He licked his fingers. "Twenty-one criminally responsible and four convicted of manslaughter – what else is there?"

Sophie would not be derailed. The clipping went back in her purse. She took another sip of her drink and continued to speak directly to Gillian. "No doubt the villain is sitting between the two of you, pushing the facts out when neither you or Karin want them. But the reality is this: since Maude began to unearth the past – it has now become my duty to see that there is someone besides those other two telling it."

"Other two?"

"The artist and the con artist." Sophie was rambling now. "He should have stayed back in Ireland or at least taken her with him somewhere, after Maude was given to your mother. Instead of life going forward after the burial of your parents, we are all taken back to the beginning of the mess."

Michel struggled to find his lighter. Sophie bit her lips. Gillian took a deep breath and waited.

"There is a new name added to the list of sympathizers every day," Michel said. "A 'who's in' and 'who was in the record,' and you can sit in this pub in the Gaspé and find out that more than half identify with either the resistance, the movements, or the FLQ but have never been directly involved. The story is 200 years old and not about to be squelched. Not even a War Measures Act will sort that out." He regarded Gillian for a moment and then abruptly took another bite of food.

Gillian could not think of a fitting reply for either one of them. She reached for her glass, took a mouthful of beer, and then quickly put the glass down again. It was obvious that Sophie felt it her duty to lay this out now, whether she could manage it or not. She would have liked to do something physical like squash Sophie like a beetle. Or since they were in the burying state, why not leave buried whatever it was that Sophie felt necessary for them to know? Instead, she heard herself say, "Lay it out there, you're going to anyway."

Sophie chose to ignore Gillian and turned towards Michel. "If you think it's about names, then you can add anybody's in this room to that list. Or anyone in or from the Gaspé, who's ever spoken to or with those that gathered around Lévesque – who by the way, has eaten dinner at my house many times. So one could easily be put in that group. I'm not talking about utopian ideologies, I'm talking about killing people."

"I'm not impressed," Michel butted his cigarette.

Sophie turned towards Gillian. "He's the mastermind. Finn Cavanagh is the one behind 1963 and he's still involved in 1970. Your mother knew it then and she never did a thing about it. She had the story, but she wanted more."

"Love. She loved him, she loved his child, isn't that why she never wrote about it?"

"Not exactly, but it's what he believes. Bloody arrogant."

"At the hospital, you made us believe they were in love," Gillian said.

"Sure they flirted back and forth – he read a lot into that, too much really. She wanted the story. It was research for her own book that got her into the tangle with him. Intelligence service and the Fenian raids – she felt she was on to something that Canadians had either forgotten or ignored. Organized intelligence for national security purposes."

"Secret agents?"

"There were a few of them. Hard to believe that in Canada but she was taken with the whole intelligence thing by accident really. She uncovered some heady material, as I said, for her own book *Guest Child*, gathering facts and details from papers about Grosse Isle – the Quarantine Station. She found some rich material from the diaries of a journalist from London. But she was never able to sort it out. Now her daughter is involved. Not completely but that's where it's going and Rousseau will make sure of that because for some reason he's determined."

"To turn his own brother in." Gillian was mesmerized.

"Call it that, I suppose." Sophie looked straight at her.

"Why haven't the police caught on to all this?"

"They won't touch him yet but they will. He's been their informant for so long now. He's feeding them all the information they need to keep control of what's going on now."

"They'll turn on him when they've got what they need – bargains will be broken." Michel got up from the table. "So what difference does it make? If it's true, they'll get him."

"The difference it makes," Gillian shot back, "is that it's my sister who's dragging us into the trouble."

"The Troubles, love, have been going on longer than this battle. Let me know when you're ready to go." He headed towards the other table to sit with the rest of the team.

Gillian caught the lighthouse beams cutting across the water. Every fifteen seconds, she remembered, the huge eye pulsed out emerald-hued flashes into the surrounding air, printing green lines on the dark surface of the water. Those signals had been a reassuring sight for generations of seamen traveling. She hadn't been up to the tower in a while. There were three in the area. In the past, she would spend hours studying the signals, pressing her nose against the glass, listening to the radio, and watching the weather patterns. Summers in the Gaspé were great when they were kids but later Murray Bay became the preference of everyone in the family but Gillian. "Too isolated," they all agreed. That was the main reason she loved the Gaspé. So she stayed with Sophie year after year, making her own rules and being left to her own entertainment. Those long, desolate summers spent on the fossil-strewn beaches and cliffs were broken at unexpected moments by the thrill of the landscape or the sight of a whale. This remoteness meant private space. That the walls were being broken through now by a trial that would link her sister, and most likely herself and Karin, with conspiracy, seemed preposterous. She got up abruptly. "I'll catch up with you tomorrow." Gillian leaned into Sophie.

"There's no way you can stop any of this from unraveling," Sophie said and moved over to join another table. "There is smoked trout in the fridge if you're still hungry when you get home."

Another round of goodbyes with the team, talk of more special projects, and promises to meet again in Percé. Gillian felt a huge relief to be outside.

"Time to get away." Michel took her arm and they walked slowly into the night along the water towards the house. A sharp wind sprung up and then silently, snow fell into the darkness. For a moment they stopped.

"That woman is determined to light fires. Don't let her get to you."

"Well she is right about one thing," Gillian said, "the story, or the truth, or whatever it is about, is all going to unravel."

He stopped and held her. "I would think it would be a relief."

She was not sure how she felt about that but somehow at this moment, she let his last remark filter the air. By the time they reached the beach house, she looked up and saw with grateful wonder, the night sky filled with stars.

Sophie's place had always held some kind of power over her.

"A house carries its own weight and also the sorrows within, the anchor between reality and desire; what we want and what we already have," Sophie once told her. What did Sophie really want? What weight or sorrow would she have residing with her?

Whatever it was, tonight the house was going to be full of desire and not much reality. Gillian had made up her mind to share the guest room. She led Michel up the stairs. The walls were papered with newsprint – stories she'd taken in summer through summer. Lace curtains hung over the windows on the landing. A small fireplace waited to be lit. There was nothing more to discuss and she wasn't certain it was about love. He would have to find his way through her, if that's what he wanted. What she wanted was to dig; to unearth whatever it was she needed to fill her. As they were about to enter the room, Gillian noticed the door to Sophie's bedroom was open. Why she went in at that particular moment…later she would ask herself that question over and over. She found herself at a table, more like a shrine, and there it was – her life – Gillian's life. What she already knew in the depths of her being was confirmed; she was in her mother's house.

karin

Here comes the hammer blow, the beginning of the never-ending saga of having to explain yourself. Out of thin air, her life was about to be reinvented. Everyone had plans for her future. There was talk about moving to the Psych ward, a place where she had once observed patients announcing their worst scenarios. Unless she agreed to time off with therapy and endless chats, like the one with the chief resident standing before her, she would be joining those detestable small groups where no one dared to talk about normal life because they had already botched that up. Karin sat up in her bed, carefully still, afraid that if she did more than breathe, the reality of what she was hearing would cause her to flinch and unravel. It could not happen. She remained poised and without a nod stared into the blue eyes of a doll-faced woman, with cropped hair the color of straw: Mireille, Chief Resident-Psychiatry.

"We have managed to miss all the signs, or maybe we saw the indicators and chose to ignore them. I mean, you know," Mireille cleared her throat, "the grief and trauma of losing your parents."

Karin listened to words like fragile and needy; no big diagnosis, she had heard them several times in the last few days. But she was not about to stop Mireille's duty to deliver the message and hand down the sentence.

"Look," Mireille started up again, "I want to tell you something, and maybe it will help you understand what I and others here are trying to say. It is a personal thing, but it happens in different ways to all of us." She began to speak slowly. "Have you ever dressed up with masks? Of course you did, I'm sure, as a child." She sat down on the bed.

"Like Halloween or costume parties. When you are young it's fun to watch others when they don't recognize you. It's strange isn't it? You know who you are with your mask on, but they don't."

She cleared her throat again, walked around, and sat down at the end of the bed this time. "Most of us walk with this guise all our lives you know – we wear those masks. And, of course, in medicine you are practically taught to do that. Only they call it detachment. Your training instills a certain scientific objectivity and distance. Anything from the heart is seen as unprofessional, or even dangerous. I worry about that sometimes, you know, that thing about connecting to the life around me." She took a breath, slid her hands down the sides of her face, and rearranged her stethoscope. "That's why we're recommending that you take some time out to work on that."

Between stunned amazement and rage, Karin responded. "But I can't, I need to work here, there's no way I can take that much time out."

"Better now than permanently out of medicine. Is that what you want?"

She didn't know.

"So, this is it," Mireille said briskly, clasping her hands together. She pushed up from the bed and headed towards the door. "I'm not about to drag it out with you. Most of us don't get second chances. You have, so grab it, take the six months and be done with it." And then she was gone.

Karin breathed deeply. Mission accomplished. Better than the psych ward, but what now – back home to Westmount? She would not waste time listening to Sophie and she couldn't face this latest frenzy with the press, like her mother's photo connected with strangers. What would Robert have said? What had he known about the past? *How little we actually know about our parents,* she thought. *How vague and undefined they are, like saints' lives —all legend unless someone takes the time to dig deeper.* She didn't want the past altered or changed but being parentless felt as though you had gone to sea in a small boat and found yourself out of sight of any shore. No longer that distant reassuring shape – nothing now between you and the horizon. No Robert telling her what to think. She resolved not to sink into that place when you wanted to curl up in the sheets, lie on your side, and watch the red numbers on the digital clock.

"I just heard." Jenny's head peered around the door. "At least they're not sacking you. Not yet anyway." She leaned over and embraced her friend. "Except you are looking like a bad piece of art. Clothes might help." She went to the small closet and reached for the leather bag that had been packed when Karin had been certain to be flying off to the Gaspé with Gillian.

"Anything interesting in here?" Jenny mused, then threw a pair of jeans and a sweater onto the bed. Her hands fumbled in her white coat pockets, then pulled out her notebook. "And after you take your time out, that puts you back on the wards, in say mid-June, in time to replace all of us wanting holidays. Nothing to it." She threw the suitcase back in the closet, sat down on the bed, and picked at the few pieces of clothing that lay in front of her.

"The strange thing is that no one believes me when I say I wasn't trying to do myself in." Karin bit her lips.

"Didn't appear that way," Jenny sighed, "and now you've only got to prove it. So stick with the plan. Free to go, check in with your mentor. Take the time and pull it together."

"While my sister has our lives splattered all over the province?"

Jenny smiled, part incredulity, part patience, and got up off the hospital bed. "Who would have known your parents were really into something big? But do you actually believe all that stuff that was written in the paper?"

"And I'm not supposed to? You knew my parents – what do you think, they were criminals?"

"Did I say that?"

"I suppose the whole hospital is talking." Karin used to trust her friend. She didn't have many and Jenny had been one of few who could put up with her. They had one thing in common that they never liked to talk about with anyone, especially medical staff – poetry and reciting works of Dickinson, Brontë, Dylan, and Cohen.

"Don't be pathetic. It's called depression. Maybe your sister has the right idea, although how would I know? Seems to me it would be the natural thing to want to know your real identity."

"Like Freud's return of the repressed – or Joseph Campbell's crossing the return threshold? How is Maude's experience going to integrate with our lives now?" Karin raised her arms over her head and cracked her knuckles.

"So you rattle your rational structures? It's better than staring out at this flat December day with the wind blowing through naked trees." Jenny drew the blind halfway down, and then pulled out her pager.

"Like Maude, digging up the family tree?"

"Why not? At least when she's crossed that threshold through her deep dark forest, she might find it easier to get on with her life." Jenny moved towards the phone on the wall but just before picking it up, she grabbed the footstool, returned to the window, and stood on it. "Returning, she re-enters life/ the way a parachutist re-enters the coarser atmosphere of earth/exchanging the sensual shapes of clouds/ for cloud-shaped trees rushing to meet her." She jumped down. "If Erickson deleted the early roots from his life and recreated himself, why can't you?"

"It was his father he chose to obliterate, not his genes. Parthenogenesis doesn't work for human beings remember?"

Jenny refused to counter, but after a silence emitted an exasperated sigh. "Anything is better than seeing you like this." In less than a minute she was gone.

Karin pulled up the sheet and closed her eyes. There were two types of people in the world, Robert used to say, those who believed in themselves and those who didn't. Before she could admit to herself which one she was today, perfume filled the room.

The duty nurse walked in, straight to the television. She turned it on and then quickly removed the sheet to grab her patient's arm. "Now they're letting them all go off to Cuba," she reported as she secured the armband to take Karin's blood pressure. "Can you believe that? Kidnap one, murder the other, and then it's off on your private aircraft to the beach in Cuba."

This morning at 8:30 a.m. the police and the army surrounded an apartment at Rue des Récollets; the street is cordoned off, schools are closed, and the inhabitants are evacuated. Fire trucks and canteens are set up and a medical team has arrived. The Cuban embassy was alerted and the Canadian pavilion at Man and His World became an extension of the embassy.

At 11:00 a.m. a negotiator, Bernard Merlger, a Montreal lawyer, entered the apartment to negotiate with the FLQ members present. They are the members of the cell that have kidnapped James Cross.

At 12:55 a.m. a 1962 Chrysler, surrounded by motorcycles and police cars and carrying three of the kidnappers, who are armed with six sticks of dynamite and two M1 semi-automatic rifles and a pistol, began its journey to the Canadian pavilion.

At 8:00 p.m. the kidnappers, along with the wife and child of one of them and two of their associates arrested earlier, are on their way to Cuba.

"Can you turn it off?" Karin protested.

The nurse gave her liquorice black curls a defiant shake, turned off the television, then ripped the band from Karin's arm. She grabbed the chart hanging at the end of the bed, scribbled, and kept her eyes focused on her notes. "It is rather sad isn't it, all this terror going on in our province? Makes you wonder how it could happen. But of course you must know more than most of us – your parents being reporters and your sister so involved." Then she repeated herself. "Must be hard for you, I mean that was your sister in the paper?"

"Look, it's like this." Karin sat up straight and recited phrase by phrase. "She was visiting this woman, an artist, her work will be showing at my aunt's gallery and what do you know – everything blows up. She's a lot like my parents, curious and wanting details and to figure things out for herself. So why did the police show up? Why question an artist? Maude was in the wrong place at the wrong time and they turn it into something else. "She...we...were brought up ..." She hesitated. "To question things, she was curious, that's all." Karin sighed deeply.

"Oh." The nurse raised her eyebrow and walked to the door. "By the way, you'll be discharged tomorrow, assuming you have some plans in place."

Karin got up and headed into the shower. She was about to have six months of freedom. What would it look like? For the first time in her life she had nothing to achieve except to follow her aunt around Paris. Steam filled the stall. She wondered what Gillian was doing now that the funeral was over – the contract with the team finished. The water turned cold as she tried to imagine that something might work out with her sister. She dried herself, wiped the mirror with the end of her towel and examined her face. The contour of her eyes was black, her skin blotchy – lips were cracked. Her eyebrows needed plucking. What a mess. Robert would be disgusted. But she wouldn't be in medicine except for Robert. She never had a choice. Her father, the intern-turned-writer, who never quite got over the rash decision that he had made when he walked out of a clinical ward never to return. And now here she was walking the path he'd left, without him.

She began a frantic search for her boots. She was certain she must have come in wearing something then remembered how she entered the hospital. She was lucky to have clothes with her. The phone rang.

"It's Gillian, are they letting you out yet?"

"Where are you? I need my boots. Yes they are letting me out, on condition I find a shrink and take some time off."

"Elle had a list of them. Michel and I are at the house in Westmount, I'll look someone up for you."

"I'm not desperate. I can find someone. What I need are my boots."

"I was talking to Maude, she's asked us to come to the gallery. Her mother, or the artist – or whatever we are supposed to call that woman, is having an exhibit. Aunt Grace organized this show long before all this happened. I think it's a good idea to go. Michel and I will fly into the Bay, we'll take you this time."

There was a knock at her door and Karin turned to Yuri Rousseau. "I'll be a minute." She motioned roughly with her finger. "Gillian." She tried to be sensitive. "Dr. Rousseau has arrived, if you want to pick me up. Whether I'm ready for the Bay and the exposition, not sure, but bring my boots."

Gillian spoke in a hush. "We may be getting more of the infamous doctor than we asked for. I'll fill you in when we pick you up."

Fill her in? It must be Maude. He had a thing going with her sister. The music festival back in fall…she had forgotten all that

– completely blanked it out. While she was busy drowning in booze and pills, both sisters were falling in love.

"How are you doing? I trust Mireille came in for a chat and that you have managed to work through some sort of plan?" He read the chart clipped at the foot of the bed and quickly signed it. If she had mildly disliked him before, the thought of having to share a future with him left her paralyzed.

"Things are coming together for me," she declared in a low voice. "I'll have a psychiatrist's name phoned in by Monday and for the time being, I'm off to stay with my aunt in Murray Bay. I thought I might consider a trip to Paris for a while. My aunt can arrange it with me."

This seemed to intrigue him, as he pulled out his pen and wrote her a prescription. "You may or may not need this," he said, handing it back to her. "I can work out some clinical time for you – only observation of course. One more thing…" as he was leaving. "You're going to have to put some weight on. But you are already aware of that, no?"

"I've always been thin and no thanks to the clinical time. If I go to Paris it will be for time out, which is what I thought I had been ordered to do. Find myself, or something like that."

The reality of Paris was unsettling. It would be far from the carefree Paris she once knew. It was too painful to even think about.

"However you wish to do so, you have a promising career before you, if you choose it."

As he moved to leave, she couldn't resist. "What about you and my sister?"

"That's not something I'm going to discuss," he replied abruptly.

She would not let go. "We've been through enough."

"Yes, well you have been an interesting example of that." He was impatient now. "But your sister seems to be finding her own way through the maze of events."

My sister, can create chaos and be admired for it, Karin thought.

maude

Anna Tougas
Paris – Québec – Maine

Someone once said that when art arrives, it opens a world and draws a crowd like a terrible accident. The evening had started as a good reason to get out on a dreary Monday, though no one would remember that. The guests arrived promptly at seven-fifteen. An event like the showing of the recent works of Anna Tougas opened up space in a dark moment, although no one could have predicted that in the spring when the gallery had booked her. But now that October had arrived in crisis, the citizens of Murray Bay were seeking a diversion from the nightly news on the television.

Whatever the reason, Maude could plainly see from her seat at the piano, that her aunt wasn't sure whether to be anxious or celebratory. The gallery was packed, people coming in from as far as Baie St. Paul, eager to socialize. Not all prospective buyers were there for a night out, like the young mayor with his mink-robed wife. And those who normally summered in Murray Bay decided that this evening adventure was worth the cold, pre-winter weekend of displacement from the big city's warmth and bright lights.

At the last minute, her aunt had decided to cater a buffet service. "Something more than a cheese log and cracker," she announced. The mini-menu turned out to be an eclectic array of cocktail meatballs, rumaki, wrapped olives, stuffed cherry tomatoes, pates, herb mushrooms, and salmon mousse. The food went down with gusto as the crowd became lively, greedily eating in the party atmosphere. Fine wines were sipped with waiters secretly anxious at the amounts consumed. Across the room were the sighs of who's who and the chatter about questions and answers – who had been questioned, who had not, and why or why not? Of the four hundred and sixty-eight arrested and held, four hundred and eight were released without charges. Amongst the group, some assumed that if you had any connections to the roundup, suddenly you were now the enemy. The *War Measures Act*, others nattered, was preposterous. Why couldn't the bureaucrats in Ottawa focus on the kidnappers, instead of interrogating the whole province? They all agreed on one thing – the autumn of the October Crisis had run its course. But it wasn't over. James Cross was free but his takers were in Cuba. Would the government send the troops to get them?

"Not to worry, they won't last on foreign soil," Aunt Grace dropped in on a group conversation. Trudeau's announcement that all military personnel, with the exception of some bodyguards, would be removed by January could not happen soon enough.

Seated at the piano, Maude played through her own version of Debussy's *L'isle Joyeuse,* while observing her aunt wandering through the crowd like an outdated movie star, trying to keep up with whatever it was that people were talking about. To have so many in the gathering must count for something. Or had the 'crisis' pushed Anna's artistic talents towards notoriety for other reasons, like the curiosity surrounding the news – the Digby connection to Anna Tougas and a certain member of the FLQ past and present. But there were no questions asked and they kept their distance from the aloof, red-headed woman sitting at the piano.

Amid the buzz, Maude sensed the unspoken speculation that the young woman making the music knew more about the FLQ than any one else in the room. She continued on with the adaptations of the *Cinq Poems de Baudelaire, Harmonie du Soire* and by the time she had completed *Le Jet d'Eau*, there was still no sign of the invited guest. As her fingers played the ivory keys, her mind swelled between the real and the imaginary. Finn with Anna, strolling in the room together, coming over to the piano, embracing her, announcing to the crowd how delighted they were to have their daughter in their midst.

In truth, he was on his way back to Ireland, or as he had so sheepishly told her, "Back to the homeland and the world of broken Irish ideologies." The last time they spoke, it was a brief conversation on the phone, long enough to make her aware of his plans.

"More like back to avoid a trial," Aunt Grace said. "As soon as this episode is over, they are going to take him in along with Theo Rousseau. They have to be realistic – sooner or later something will happen to them…that is if they don't wind up dead first." She spoke with a voice designed to alarm.

Her aunt, like Sophie, was competing as family historian. Grace was determined now to get the facts straight for her brother's children. Some of it Maude had heard as a child but had never paid much attention. She remembered Robert telling them some days about Sophie's past lives and the fact that she had been an informant at one time, but now Maude wondered if it was true. Except now it mattered because Maude was tied to Finn and Anna; connected through the campaigns, the political protests, and then the killing. They had underestimated the severity of their actions and the complexity of it all. Or had they? And then there was Elle. Her mother couldn't defend herself now or answer the bigger part of the puzzle, which was why the police were not arresting Finn.

"They will. It's a matter of timing. They wait it out and when they've got everyone, they will bring him in. Obviously a deal's been made," Aunt Grace explained. "Sophie's most likely been keeping them informed."

That others were sifting through the details of a past life where she supposedly now belonged made it sound all the more fictitious. Even Yuri had his chance to clarify some of those details. He never tried. Instead he let her fumble her way through the confusion. "They say that the bomb went off before they realized the old guy was still there," he said about the night watchman.

"But they claimed the FLQ was responsible?"

"The cause was obviously more important at the time, I guess." He had said this with indifference. She remembered that at the time, she had wondered how calculatedly his words were phrased. She hadn't expected to see him after that. It was a mistake, she thought, to feel like she could have some kind of relationship with someone who couldn't tell her the truth about himself, unless, he was protecting his older brother.

The room, it seemed, had become claustrophobic. She needed a break from the piano. Guests were full after the gourmet gorging and the buzz from the wine was fading. The previously animated discussions were leaning towards the mundane. And still no sight of Anna. The art critics were putting away their notebooks, apparently resigned to the fact there would be no live interviews or questions for the artist.

Maude was scanning the crowd, looking for some way to exit, when her sisters arrived with Michel. Not only did they break the monotony now shrouding the room, they were her first contact that evening with anyone besides her aunt.

Gillian approached the piano first. Her trademark, the ponytail, was now replaced with a cropped bob. And her lips were no longer pale and natural. But the biggest difference was, she was smiling. Michel looked different from that first day when he'd strolled into the gallery although she wasn't sure yet what it was. It seemed that everyone else around her had changed, even her older sister, although Maude couldn't tell if it was for the worse or better.

"I know what you're thinking," Karin said, spreading her thin arms. Her diminishing body was now so apparent. "Come closer, I won't break," her breath faintly touching Maude's face. "Has Yuri asked you to marry him yet?"

Maude smiled automatically, relieved to be away from the piano but not out of the clutch of her sister, who pressed in with more on the romantics. "Gillian's obviously smitten. And the last social outing we had together, I remember you were very keen on the doctor."

A waiter approached with a tray of wine. They eagerly reached for a glass.

"Quite the group here," Gillian interrupted, "but where is the guest of honour? I've never seen the place so full at one time."

"Would anyone be here if it wasn't for our sister and Anna?" Karin circled her hand with disgust towards the paintings.

"By the way, thanks for turning us into a province-wide showcase." Karin surveyed the room, and added, "It's about you and her, or why would they be here?"

If Maude had mumbled something about filling in the pieces of the puzzle – what some had termed genealogical bewilderment… that would never adequately explain to either of her sisters why she had contacted her biological mother.

"I've never seen so many in Murray Bay," Gillian interrupted, "in the same place."

"Would any of them be here if it wasn't for our darling sister?" Karin insisted.

"You're not still harping on that are you?" Gillian defended. "It's done now and to be honest, I'm starting to think that it might be a good thing for Maude and us."

"You mean she had it all but thought life would have been better with these two terrorists." Karin kept her eyes fixed on the paintings.

"Put aside your own feelings for once and see it for what it is. She did a search, found a messy set up, and now be thankful she wasn't part of it," said Gillian.

Gillian had always been very good at placing things neatly where they belonged. It didn't matter if she never understood or even tried to, as long as things were placed. She wouldn't hear that the trace was never about choosing, or preferences, nor would she grasp or want to accept that it was about the knowing. Knowing was the one thing Gillian or Karin did not want and it was the only reason Maude had gone to all the bother in the first place. Maybe that had changed, although for now, Gillian couldn't bring herself to talk about it.

By nine-thirty p.m. nothing had been purchased. Some headed for the coat rack. Aunt Grace made a few calls but no one could confirm the whereabouts of the artist. Then, without anyone really aware of how quickly it happened, the police arrived; half a dozen officers and plainclothes infiltrated the room, questioning and seeking any kind of information that might give clues as to the whereabouts of FLQ members and support networks. At least that's what everyone was told.

"Ottawa is obviously not in tune with Québec." Michel reappeared. "They're going to play this out for as long and for all they can get."

Aunt Grace was devastated. "No one will ever come back. I'm ruined. That's all they'll remember, coming here to the art show and being interrogated."

Some actually believed Finn would show up. But neither he nor Anna appeared and by eleven the place was empty. The police left without any arrests; no one. The guests left without buying any artwork.

"If your mother was here, none of this would have happened," Aunt Grace sniffled, as her nieces tried to console her over the loss of sales. "She was good at handling these kinds of things. She would definitely have taken care of those horrid police officers."

"They wouldn't have gotten in the door," Karin's eyes rolled at her sisters, as she helped her aunt into the car.

Gillian, Michel, and Maude returned to the house. Driving through the dark night, they were too tired to speak. Under normal circumstances, Gillian would have had strong opinions and run through the events with a summary that would startle them all at their own lack of perception. For a few brief moments, Maude wished that Gillian would rant, to bring things back to some sense of normal. But you don't see things the same way, in the backseat of a car, half asleep under the arm of a man old enough to be your father. What did she care about at this point, Maude thought as she stole a glance at the contented couple through the rear view mirror, while fighting the need for sleep. She steered down the gravel road and into the driveway of the little house that had once taken her breath away.

The call came from Finn in the morning. "She's gone."

The facts, as far as they could be ascertained, were sketchy. A concerned poet who had been writing some pieces to accompany Anna's work had alerted the police. At first, they went through her house and found nothing unusual. Only that Anna, who was not an extraordinary housekeeper, had left her paints tightly sealed, brushes cleaned, and no signs of disorder. No one had really seen her leave her row house or had heard from her for several days. She had become reclusive and there were few people who observed her coming and going.

Several students from L'École des Beaux Arts, who sold her work along le Rue des Trésors, were questioned.

"She's missed several appointments with clients," they said. "That's unusual for someone dependent on money like she is, but she leads her own life."

"Cuba," Finn called a second time to confirm her whereabouts.

"An impulsive whim maybe, she was capable of doing strange things. She's left an envelope. It will be delivered to you later today." That was all he said and Maude felt it was pointless to ask more questions. Later, she wondered how it came about that he knew all the details so accurately. It took several days, before the story came out. This time, Gillian would not let her read the newspaper or watch television. When the letter from Anna arrived Maude couldn't open it.

It seemed that everyone was making offers. The Digby girls needed help. Sophie wanted Gillian to move to the Gaspé – Karin and Maude would be welcome.

"It won't happen. We're planning a trip to Pennsylvania," Gillian announced placing her hands on Michel's shoulders.

"Deep Pennsylvania," he corrected.

"Digging for fossils in cornfields and farmlands. Apparently they've blasted into rocks and found fish bones," she repeated, "and the rocks are so crammed with them they've named the place Big Fish Alley. And then we are off to South Africa, something a little more exotic, to do some underwater work on lobefins."

Karin decided to stay in Murray Bay with her aunt. "We'll be going to Paris together, although I don't relish the idea of seeing it with a seventy-five year old. At least she won't be coming to the

Medical Research Institute. I have to do something to keep my studies going. Rousseau's arranged it for me."

Like the bee's electric sting, Maude cringed but bounced back as the announcement from her sister so out of character made it ridiculously sound like Paris would be just what the doctor ordered. They laughed for the first time since the accident of their parents.

Maude was the only one prepared to go back to Westmount, although she felt she could no longer predict anything or make any plans.

"What will you do?" Finn asked on his next call.

Had she made her own inquiries regarding 'pseudo cells,' he wanted to know.

"Not really," she said.

"What does that mean?" He pressed for more information.

In a sudden rush she told him, "Sophie seems to have explained all that and, of course, the good doctor."

"Yes," he sighed. "I imagine they have."

"How can informants have so much protection?" she asked. "And why?"

"It's not in the way you think," he replied abruptly.

"But what about the kidnappers? Getting away with murder."

"They'll be back in no time and then the lot of them will be arrested. Plus others." He didn't mention Anna.

"And the night watchman at McGill?"

"Yes, I was there, things went wrong."

"Is that why you agreed to…"

He interrupted her now. "You've been told too many stories. I've more than made up for that incident. And I wasn't the one to ignite the bomb, neither was Theo."

Later that week, driving back along the highway towards Québec City, Maude listened to the interview between the Solicitor-General and the Justice Minister from Ottawa.

"The police know that members of the FLQ are getting ready for more action, but they know the members of those cells. They are kept very well informed and have in their possession a whole series of clues. The Solicitor-General added that some of the information available to him could not be revealed. But the Justice Minister was determined. Terrorist incidents will be nipped in the bud, thanks to the work of the secret police agents."

The roads were icy and Maude was too nervous to continue past Québec City. She would stay in a room for the night until the highway was clear. But she had one stop to make. As she entered the city, she glanced out the car window to the army trucks parked on the side of the road. The soldiers were young…boys, not much older than she was, although she felt she had aged at least ten years on them. Automatic rifles hanging from their shoulders, as natural and normal as anything else they might do. Did they understand anything about the *War Measures Act*?

She drove through Grand Allée and turned onto the side street where Anna lived. The police had cordoned off a section making it impossible to park in front of her house. After driving through the narrow streets of Old Québec, she found parking and then walked slowly towards the small crowd milling around the area. Yuri emerged from a side street in jeans, a t-shirt, and leather jacket. Maude felt the tension in her body, then a dizzying pang to escape.

"I'm on my way home," she said quietly.

"Home?"

"Yes, strange isn't it? All I want to do is return to Westmount, back to the Circle." Her eyes searched past him to the small crowd gathered in front of Anna's townhouse. She wondered who they would be. She hadn't considered that Anna might have had her own group of friends.

"That's an awfully large house for one person," he moved towards her.

Tears came but now she was herself again, who ever that was – Maude Digby.

"There will be a trial," she said.

"Some day. Don't hold your breath. Life goes on."

"What about you?" She reached for his hand.

"Back to the war, where the work is. That won't change."

"Karin may end up with you some day, out there on the field."

"Not if I can help it." His eyes held that fixed gaze that had drawn her to him the first time they met. "Keep up with your music." He reached for her now. "Medicine needs you."

"I'm leaving that," she smiled. "I noticed my need to ask questions. Elle…" She cleared her throat. "My mother used to say that journalists are like troublesome children, asking too many questions." She put her hand to her forehead then moved sideways. "I want something in there, just one thing. Do you think they'll let me in?"

"Are you sure?"

"I have to."

The wind shifted and it began to snow.

Yuri went towards the police, who were watching Maude as she made her way towards the entrance of Anna's house. One of the officers motioned to let her go in.

Without any hesitation she walked through the door, past the paints and canvas boards, and up the stairs to the guest room where she had spent that one night with Anna. She entered the room slowly. Anna, Finn, and Elle, were smiling at her. She removed the photo from the dresser, took another picture this time in her mind, and moved slowly out of Anna's home into the snow-filled night.

charlotte

2001

Crossing the Return Threshold is one of the most innovative though not so dynamic documentaries this year, especially now that the Referendum is over. It attempts to balance problems of politics, culture, nationalism, terrorism, motherhood, identity, and death, with clearly not a boundary between them. The October Crisis ended in 1970, when tanks rolled through the streets of the province of Québec and people were arrested without charge. Given that this film takes place just as the revolution was ending, Rousseau's assessment of that period is confusing. All that bother, Charlotte Rousseau seems to be saying, and this is what you wind up with: a cultural scene that depends on some totally imagined vision of the French motherland and a young woman who has almost nothing in the way of personal identity, national self, or meaningful relationships.

"Have you seen it?" a male voice asked.

"What?"

"Crossing the Return Threshold."

"Why?"

"I read the review before you had a chance to get it," he said before I answered. "The magazine was handed to me first. Not many Americans know about the October Crisis. I'm Josh," he said, as his hand extended to me in a manner I considered rather forward for two strangers sharing airspace.

What is it about planes that gives a person the liberty to bluntly ask you things that they would never ask elsewhere?

"Charlotte Rousseau," I reply, shaking his hand.

He smiles and leans towards the paper with intensity. "Nice. Québec or France?"

"It's a long story," I said.

I am less inclined to talk about names and histories, for fear of favouring one over the other, or taking any of them too close to the heart. I was tired…overtired, my bones ached and my round protruding belly was putting enormous pressure on my right side. Shifting my body would have been welcomed. Instead, I continued to stare at the critic's review in the *Montreal Star*. Everything should have been resolved after Maude, my mother, found her mother and father and figured out her birth issues. But it was not the end and since I had come along, it seemed I should be the one to complete the story.

"Are you a teacher?" Josh persisted.

"Documentaries."

"Really, that's different. So what about this one, have you seen it?"

"What if I told you that I wrote the script and that the woman in the film, the one the critic refers to as 'possessing almost nothing in the way of personal identity or national self' was my mother? It's her story."

"Everything?"

"Pretty much. It's not easy to explain or understand. But it wasn't true that they had no identity, of course they did, maybe, they weren't sure where they belonged. That is what my mother would say."

My plane partner was silent.

It took ten years after the October Crisis before my grandfather, Finn, and my uncle Theo, finally went to trial. No one ever understood why it took so long, except that they would say – they had to be connected. The great mystery was protecting Finn for the sake of another's identity. It came out in the papers that it was possible that Finn had been recruited by the Anti-Terrorist section of our government to work as an informant; a peculiar idea to understand or even believe in this country. He was also hired to protect Sophie's involvement with the pseudo cells. She was part of the group that belonged to the phony FLQ. She had always wanted my mother and her sisters to know the truth behind the movements. She also wanted Gillian to know she was her mother. Gillian figured it out for herself. All truth comes to the surface in time. Another argonauta washed up one day in the Gaspé and revealed so much about motherhood than either Sophie or Gillian were able to express in words. In truth, my mother would say, she wasn't sure if Sophie loved Finn or my mother, but she loved Gillian more than either of them.

Eventually, my uncle received one year in prison and my grandfather, I guess you could call him that – nothing. Anna's name or story never appeared in print before or after the trial. It had been ten years since Anna had run off to Cuba. My mother told me that the letter written to her from Anna, when she darted off to Cuba during the Crisis, revealed she had turned informant for Ottawa several years after my mother's birth.

When the trial started, my father wanted me shipped off to France to be out of Québec and the public eye. My mother disagreed. She was so intent on breaking that family secret syndrome. She had to.

Finn's trial was the catalyst that perforated the already wounded heart of my mother. Those were my father's words, although he wasn't there to support her – off to another war, something he could never give up, not for my mother, not for me. Even though I was young, I'd like to think it was because I was mature for my age that she poured it all out like a mighty flowing river that had been blocked but that wasn't it. One day she was crying, and she couldn't stop.

"Charlotte, thank you for caring. Right now there's just no one else to talk to."

In reality she had no choice, not only because she wanted me to know the story but because years later, during the referendum in 1995 when she told me that "yes" was her vote, it finally hit me how much her life was entrapped by this identity thing. I sided with the "no" – no to separation of any kind.

After the referendum, on one unusually bright and warm fall day, Karin, Gillian, and my mother Maude reunited in Murray Bay. There, over a conciliatory bottle of Viognier, the sisters, each exhausted with the identity struggle – personal and political – agreed enough was enough.

"A toast," my aunt Karin pronounced. "To a proper start."

"That's what we were given," Gillian added, and my mother agreed. "A family."

acknowledgements

excerpt from *Gift from the Sea* by Anne Morrow Lindberg, copyright ©1955, 1975, copyright renewed 1983 by Anne Morrow Lindberg. Used by permission of Pantheon Books, an imprint of the Knopf Doubleday Publishing Group, a division of Random House LLC. All rights reserved.

Special thanks to author Ron Graham, who granted permission to depict life as it was in Westmount from *The French Quarter*. Author and translator Edward Baxter, kindly agreed permission to use the communiqués from his book *FLQ Anatomy of an Underground Movement*. Palaeontologist Jim Haggart helped me understand the dynamics on an archaeological dig and the need for a proper burial. Jo McClelland from *The Glass Coin* asked valuable questions about the characters. Ruth Fluevog, along with her pencil, read and endured draft 3. Glen Phillips, my husband, has lovingly supported this book for five years.

The characters in this novel are fictional although set during one of the most dramatic political events in Canadian history. This story was birthed while dining at L'été in the region of Charlevoix. Time spent in the Gaspé allowed me to connect with the landscape and the stories that a house can tell.

reference sources

Balcom, Karen. *The Ideal Maternity Home*, <u>Acadiensis</u>, Spring 2002

Dube, Philippe. *Charlevoix Two Centuries at Murray Bay,* McGill-Queen's University Press, Kingston & Montreal London Buffalo, 1990

Fournier, Louis. Translation by Edward Baxter, *FLQ The Anatomy of an Underground Movement,* NC Press Limited, Toronto, 1984

Graham, Ron. *The French Quarter.* Macfarlane Walter & Ross. Toronto, 1992.

Grescoe, Taras. "Where fishes walked." Canadian Geographic. 1997 (Gillian's background recording Chapter 3)

Hill, Michael. "Archaeologists reconstruct life of 18th century skeleton" Nando Media

LePage, Robert. *No.* Canadian Film & Review, cited in Charlotte's film review – fictional '*Crossing the Return Threshold*'

Lifton, Betty Jean. *Twice Born*. McGraw-Hill Book Company. New York, St. Louis, San Francisco, Toronto, Mexico and Dusseldorf. 1975

Pastan, Linda. *Waiting for My Life*, "Returning" W.W. Norton & Company, New York, New York. 1981 (poetry cited in Chapter 8)

Toolis, Kevin. *Rebel Hearts, Journeys within the IRA's Soul*, St. Martin's Press, New York, 1995

The Canadian Press. "Tourist Baby Survives Unusual Pregnancy" 11 August, 2003 www.canada.com/montreal/story (cited in Karin's description of the rare ectopic pregnancy)

Printed in Canada